D1515213

Gunman's Justice

Gunman's Justice

P.A. BECHKO

Sagebrush
Large Print Westerns

Library of Congress Cataloging in Publication Data

Bechko, P.A.
  Gunman's justice / P.A. Bechko.
  p.   cm.
  ISBN 1-57490-012-9 (alk. paper)
  1. Large type books. I. Title.
[PS3552.E24G86   1996]
813'.54—dc20   96-19290
                                                  CIP

Cataloguing in Publication Data is available from
the British Library and the National Library of Australia.

Sagebrush Large Print Westerns are published in the
United States and Canada by Thomas T. Beeler, Publisher,
Box 659, Hampton Falls, New Hampshire 03844-0659.
ISBN 1-57490-012-9

Published in the United Kingdom, Eire, and the Republic of
South Africa by Isis Publishing Ltd, 7 Centremead, Osney
Mead, Oxford OX2 0ES England. ISBN 0-7531-5132-4

Published in Australia and New Zealand by Australian
Large Print Audio & Video Pty Ltd, 17 Mohr Street,
Tullamarine, Victoria, 3043, Australia. ISBN 1-86340-588-7

Manufactured in the United States of America

Gunman's Justice

CHAPTER ONE

The air was crisp and cool, it made a man feel good just to breathe it. Thorne Stevens pulled up on the crest of a high hill and let the big gray horse of his blow while he had himself a good look around. It was a clear day this fall of 1887. There wasn't any chance of snow, at least not soon. Ahead, the land stretched out green and rolling, and laced with swift flowing creeks. In the distance, mountains thrust their jagged peaks into the blueness of the sky. It wasn't hard, even from where Thorne sat his horse, one leg hooked up around the saddle horn, to pick out the broad expanse of snow that blanketed the slopes of the mountains in vast fields. This was the Wind River country in the wild, free territory of Wyoming and Thorne Stevens felt like he was coming home.

Just past thirty, Thorne Stevens was looking for a place to stop his drifting. Standing past the six-foot mark, he was a tall man with broad, timber-cutting shoulders, and narrow, trail-rider's hips. His face had the tanned, weathered look of an outdoor man. Hands that were big with squared-off fingers, and had not gone hardly a day without knowing hard physical labor, rolled a cigarette with the dexterity of a fine craftsman. Light brown hair that was both curly and shaggy showed from beneath the brown Stetson he wore pushed back on his head. Thorne relaxed in the saddle while he smoked and gazed about himself. There wasn't much those snapping blue-gray eyes of his missed. Narrow eyebrows the color of his hair arched high above his eyes, and the high cheekbones he'd gotten from his father's side of the family gave those eyes a look that made most men think twice before doing anything to cross him.

In spite of the cool, fall air, the heavy green jacket that Thorne wore hung open as did his black leather vest, and the black shirt he wore underneath them. Thick hair, a couple of shades darker than that on his head, spilled from the unbuttoned shirt front. The pants he wore were black as his shirt, the down-at-heel boots were covered with trail dust and his tan leather gloves had seen more than their day of work. A cream-colored neckerchief he wore was in odd contrast to the rest of his dark-colored clothing. It had been a gift. A gift from a woman he had known, but that had been a long time ago.

A sharp rustling in the brush caused Thorne's hand to drop automatically to the Colt .44 Peacemaker that rode at his hip. He had been drifting up one side of the country and down the other, and one thing he had learned first, was that it paid a man to be careful. The big gray Thorne rode gave a welcoming whinny as a brute of a dog came through the low brush growling nearby to drop at the horse's side panting from his run. Thorne relaxed, throwing a few low words in the dog's direction. Jake, as Thorne had named the dog, was a cross between a wolf and a dog. He looked a lot like a wolf, but was much bigger than any wolf Thorne had ever seen. Jake had a thick ruff, distinctive black markings, and coat that looked almost blue, it was so gray. Thorne and Jake had been together for nearly six years. He had taken the wolf-dog by force from a man who had been beating him. Jake hadn't been quite a year old at the time, and Thorne wasn't a man who could stand by while an animal was mistreated. He and Jake had been traveling partners ever since, and a more loyal, fighting dog a man

2

couldn't ask for.

When Thorne saw that Jake was rested, he snubbed out his smoke on his saddle horn and started down the north side of the hill, leading his pack horse behind. Jake sprang to his feet and trotted easily alongside the gray. There were a lot more miles to be covered. Thorn had been through this country once before, almost eleven years before, back in '76, and he knew it wouldn't be long before he reached that mountain valley he had been dreaming about. The way Thorne figured it, he'd done enough hellraising, and now he was ready to settle down. He rode down the steep hillside with a steadying hand on the gray guiding him expertly, while at the same time he kept the pack horse's line free of knots as it scrambled down behind them. Thorne was a down-to-earth-type man, and there wasn't much that either man or nature hadn't thrown at him at one time or another. It had not taken him long to acquire his cynical outlook on life. That, combined with an explosive temper, and an equal ability with either fists or guns, had given him a reputation from as far south as the Rio Grande to as far north as the Powder River. There had been a short time quite a few years back when Thorne had half appreciated that reputation, but he had gained considerable intelligence since then. He was planning on starting himself a little spread up in the high mountains, just as far away from other folks as he could get. For a spell, the only company he wanted was Jake and the big gray he rode.

Thorne eased his mount into a long, ground-eating lope, and the big dog and pack animal had no trouble in keeping up. Meadows rolled out at the horse's feet, green and lush despite the lateness of the season. Clumps of trees were scattered here and there, but Thorne swung around them. He had a goal, and he wasn't going to sidetrack until he reached it.

The meadows were left behind, and the high mountains rose all around Thorne as he began picking his way up a slope, his eyes searching for the trail he remembered from so long ago. He wasn't real good at remembering the names of mountains and passes and such, for Thorne had traveled a lot of rough country, but he never forgot a landmark or a pass, nor did he ever forget a face. Carefully, he crossed country he had seen only once before, pushing on for a valley he knew lay cupped in the hollow of the mountains before him. It had not been an easy trip this far, and he had gotten nearly to his destination later in the year than he would have liked. Before winter set in hard, there was a lot that would have to be done. Shelters had to be put up for himself as well as for the horses, supplies had to be laid in, and the range checked. A man had to know his own country to be sure of himself.

The air was taking on a damp chill and it was as only a couple hours from sunset when Thorne found what he had been looking for. The earth here was fan-shaped and dotted with large rocks and tall pines. It narrowed farther up ahead like a funnel, until there was room on the trail for no more shall three horses abreast. The trail was bordered on one side by a sheer drop and on the other by a rock wall that rose above the trail with the same abruptness as the drop on the other side. There would be snow up ahead. There was hardly ever a time when there wasn't snow in the pass. Later, when the blizzards hit the high country, it would be impassable. It would be a matter of months before a man could use it. Thorne half smiled as he started up the pass. It

4

would not be long, until he was completely cut off from other men, and that was the way he wanted it. Once the winter snows settled in, his place could not even be stumbled on by accident. But at the other end of the narrow pass, where the trail dipped down for better than a thousand feet, widening only a little as it led into his valley, the winter would be much less severe. Heavy snowstorms swirled around the high peaks surrounding the valley, but comparatively little of it ever reached the floor of the valley. There would still be heavy drifts and a long winter, but this hidden spot was better off than most of the ranches that clung to the foot of the mountains.

Pushing on, Thorne glanced once again at the sun. He would not be able to make it through the pass before dark, and he did not know it well enough to try the rocky grades and sharp turns in the dark. If he remembered correctly, there was a place a short piece up ahead, just before the trail narrowed where a man could camp if he did not mind a rock ledge. If he camped there for the night, Thorne planned on being in the valley before noon the next day. He rode easy, thinking of the days ahead. There would be hard work, plenty of it. There was a lot to getting a spread started, even one as small as he figured to be starling with. There should be some wild stuff running loose up there, if he remembered right, and nobody saw fit to take them. There had been quite a few ragtag cattle up here the last time he passed this way. They were offspring from the cattle the Indians had stolen years ago from the settlers. They had been wild and ornery as all get out, but cattle nonetheless, and Thorne figured he could slap a brand on anything wearing horns, hoofs, and hide.

5

The night came and went quickly with nothing to show for its passing save a chill wind that moaned softly through the pass. Thorne buttoned his shirt and tied his vest closed across it. The coat still hung open. Before he started down the far side it would be getting considerably colder, that Thorne knew for a fact. It would probably be snowing higher up— Thorne could feel it in the wind. He had never felt the cold much. That was probably the reason he liked the high country with its frosty peaks and open vastness better than anything he had ever seen.

He broke camp before first light and pulled out as soon as the sun was high enough to light the trail. Jake before the gray Thorne rode with head held high, trotted and sniffing the air, always eager to see what was up ahead. The gray was as used to rough country as was the pack horse. Both had been with him for better than two years. They took to the trail like they were heading for green pasture, following the dips and cutbacks like mountain goats.

The narrow trail crested at a rocky ledge overlooking the sprawling valley below. Thorne pulled up a few minutes, letting his eyes wander over the untouched wilderness that spread out from beneath his horse's feet. It was still the same as the picture Thorne had carried around in his mind during the past years. The rich green grass was thick and rolling far below like a restless sea. The valley was long and oval like an immense gravy boat. Towering mountain peaks rose majestically on all sides to stand in stark relief against the blueness of the sky. A stream, bubbling and foaming, threaded its way through the valley like a bit of ribbon carelessly thrown with no thought as to where it might land. Its glistening length reached back far into the distant mountains. Tall stands of pines grew on the higher slopes surrounding the valley, along with alder, birch, and mountain mahogany. Along the stream on the valley floor were some willow and poplar. Scattered off toward the mountains were an occasional stand of aspen. There were no wildflowers now, but in the spring when Thorne had first set eyes on this place they had carpeted the valley with a brilliant splash of color. Thorne took a deep breath and started the gray down the remainder of the rocky trail. Here a man could breathe easy. There was plenty of room to grow. It would take time, probably a lot of it, but Thorne was sure he would see the day when that green valley would be dotted with his own grazing cattle, maybe some horses too. It didn't take much effort for him to imagine a cabin on one of those green slopes from where he could keep a careful eye on his stock. Before the first snows fell, that cabin would be started. There wouldn't be much need for fences, except maybe up at the trail. Another way out of the valley on foot was a possibility, but Thorne had not come across any other trail a horse could take the first time he had been in the valley.

It felt good to be riding, to feel the big gray moving smoothly beneath him, and to know he was starting a new life. A man couldn't see the future, but the way Thorne felt, breathing that mountain air, and coming smartly down the sloping trail, he could even imagine a wife to go along with that little cabin, and maybe, in time, a son to pass the spread on to.

What had changed him, Thorne could not clearly remember. Maybe he just hadn't really been what folks figured him to be in the first place. He had killed, more times than he liked to think about. He had never gone hunting it, but he had never backed down either. Things might have been a lot easier if he had.

By the time Thorne reached the stream that flowed through the valley, he was well past ready for a drink from its mountain-cooled waters. He stepped from the saddle, letting the big gray and pack animal drink downstream while he laid down on the bank to drink. Jake trotted on ahead, seeming to be more eager to taste the air than the water. Thorne took off his hat, drinking deeply of the sweet, cold water, then splashed it over his face and neck. After the long miles Thorne had covered, even the shock of the icy water felt good to his skin.

Jake's peculiar half bark half howl drifted back to Thorne from farther upstream where the willows clustered along the streambank. It wasn't like Jake to get himself all het up over nothing so Thorne slapped his hat back on his head and took out to see what had set Jake off. With the caution of an experienced man, he moved upstream rapidly. Habits were something a man lived with and he didn't really know what to expect. Habit was what made him draw his Colt as he moved toward the dog.

When Thorne came up on Jake, the big dog was alone, but he was sniffing with a little more than casual interest at the edge of the streambank where the grasses were matted down. Thorne looked intently at the surrounding area. There were some crimson blotches staining the grass. It was blood. Thorne had seen enough of it to know, and he didn't figure it was animal blood neither. The thick grasses were still pretty well crushed to the ground. Thorne had read a lot of sign, and what he saw in front of him was as plain as printing on a page. Somebody else was in this valley, somebody who was hurt bad,

8

from the looks of it, and somebody who didn't want to be found. Whoever had been drinking from the stream had been interrupted by the arrival of Thorne, and headed for cover. Butting into someone else's business wasn't something Thorne took lightly to, but this was something different. Whoever had been here before him was hurt pretty bad, might be bleeding to death. The fact that whoever it was did not want to be found, gave Thorne reason to decide he was dodging trouble, and that was one thing Thorne could do without. Besides, Thorne wasn't much on surprises. If there was some hombre spilling blood all over his valley, he wanted to know who it was. Whoever the stranger was, he had been hurt, and at this spot only minutes ago. It was not likely he could have gone far in that short a time.

"Go find him, Jake," Thorne urged to the already eager dog.

Jake took one last sniff in the crushed grass and willows then lit out, covering ground in long even strides. Holstering his gun, Thorne ran back the short distance to collect the horses. The sun was near straight overhead and there was a cool breeze drifting across the valley floor. Stepping into the saddle, Thorne let the gray lope until he caught up with Jake. The big dog had stopped short where the ground started to rise. Some good-sized boulders were up ahead, and some pine strung along the slope, angling up the mountain. Jake was ready to take out again as soon as Thorne had caught up to him, but Thorne stopped him with a word. The way Jake stared up at those rocks Thorne knew that would be where the stranger was holed up. It was the only cover close to the stream. He stepped down and tied the horses to a sprig of a pine tree that was trying to get a start in the valley. Easing himself around the horses, Thorne moved toward where a swell in the ground could provide some protection, if there was any shooting. If that stranger was still conscious, after losing all that blood, Thorne guessed he would be sitting up there in them rocks holding a gun on him. That's what he'd be doing right now if their positions were reversed.

A bullet snapped through the air and kicked up dirt at Thorne's boot toe. He dropped to the ground and rolled over behind the protection of the rise. Jake had been in enough scrapes with Thorne to know what it meant when he heard a gun go off. The big dog laid down behind some rocks considerably closer to the gunman than Thorne. Thorne had his gun out, but for the moment he didn't want to use it. Seemed to him that the gunman was either an awful poor shot, or else he hadn't aimed to hit him in the first place. It might be that the stranger wasn't quite sure about him.

It was going to take a little planning, but Thorne aimed to get himself up in the rocks to find out what was going on. It didn't seem sensible to get himself shot doing it though. Jake was over by the rocks bristling, knowing the gunshot for an attack on his master. Bellying over to the farthest end of the bump in the earth that was shielding him, Thorne estimated the sprint from where he lay to the first rocks as not more than twenty-five feet. He settled his battered brown Stetson a little firmer on his head and shrugged out of his heavy, sheepskin-lined jacket so he could move easier. He gave Jake a hand signal that started the big dog skulking up that rock-strewn slope like a wolf moving in for the kill.

Lunging to his feet, Thorne ran for the rocks only a few feet away. A shot cracked through the air and

10

slammed into the dirt close enough to Thorne's heel for him to feel the shock of it hitting the earth. He sprawled out behind some rocks, but with hardly a pause, scrambled back to his feet, picking his way quickly up the low slope. One more shot split the air as he climbed, glancing off a rock with a piercing whine. Either that fella up in those rocks didn't believe in wasting bullets or he didn't have any to spare. Jake came to the top of one of the larger boulders with an easy, catlike jump and growled low in his throat.

For an instant the man up in the rocks had his attention on the dog, crouched low, and looking more menacing than a winter-starved wolf. His gun swung toward Jake as Thorne came up through the line of pines from the side. Jake came up off that rock above the young stranger like a bobcat, bowling him over as he hit the ground and knocking his gun a couple of feet out of his reach. There was a look of grim determination on the young man's face as he gave a desperate lunge for his gun.

All the blood Thorne had seen had been coming from the leg of the stranger, and he hadn't quite gripped the gun butt when Thorne clipped him on the chin, knocking him cold. His job finished, Jake dropped to the ground, quietly watching his master as he moved about the small hollow. He panted lightly, and his ears remained pricked forward, always alert.

Thorne picked the gun up from the ground and tucked it into his own belt. He hadn't wanted to hit the young man that way, but it was the quickest way he knew to get things settled. He looked down at the unconscious young man at his feet as he stepped across him. He was dark, with black hair that was thick and unruly. The eyes would be brown, set deep

11

beneath heavy black eyebrows. He was young, probably not more than twenty and his face still had a soft look about it, in spite of the grim lines that were deep about his eyes and mouth. His build was slender, and there wasn't much obvious muscle on his frame. Despite his appearance, Thorne knew that if he had worked on a ranch at all, he was a strong boy.

Taking a knife from his boot, Thorne slit open the young man's pants leg to get a good look at the wound. It was easy to see why the bleeding hadn't stopped. The slug was still in there. Thorne let his breath out in a long sigh. With all the work there was to be done before winter, he gets saddled with this kid, and whatever trouble there was dogging his heels. From a coldly realistic point of view, Thorne knew a body didn't get shot up like that accidentally while he was cleaning his gun. Experience told him that if a man was worth shooting, he was worth killing. If that past experience was any way to tell, Thorne knew it wouldn't be too long before he had somebody down his neck looking to finish the job he'd started. Retying the neckerchief the wounded young man had tied over the wound, Thorne eased his weight across his own broad shoulders and started down the slope. That leg needed doctoring, but Thorne didn't think it would cause too much trouble once the bullet was out, and he had dug out his share. There wasn't any way of telling whether this one deserved what he got, or if maybe the law had put that bullet where it was, but Thorne never had been one to sidestep trouble. At least, not if it meant giving into the threat of another man's gun. It was said the number of times Thorne Stevens backed down could be counted on one hand.

Reaching the horses, Thorne laid the wounded

man across his own saddle and walked the horses over to where he was going to set up camp in the trees near the stream. Throwing a camp together, he dug out the bullet and bandaged the man's leg from things he was carrying in his supplies. Thorne was the kind of man who never hit a trail without plenty to tend to whatever might come up. The slug had been in plenty deep, wedged right up against the thigh bone high on his right side. It was only luck that the leg wasn't broken. During the whole thing the wounded man never opened his eyes. He had to have lost a lot of blood to be that weak. Finishing up, Thorne made the stranger as comfortable as he could, and glanced about. He could not have come into the valley without a horse, and that meant it had to be running free somewhere, probably not far away. Thorne glanced up at the sun. If he meant to find that horse before nightfall, he would have to be moving pretty fast.

As Thorne started for his horse, Jake came to his feet and trotted alongside, looking up at him expectantly. Grinning at the big dog's eagerness, Thorne shook his head. "Watch him," he told the big dog quietly.

Jake wheeled and trotted back the few steps to where the wounded stranger lay, dropping in the grass a short distance from him. He dropped his massive head on his forepaws and heaved a long sigh as Thorne stepped into the leather and rode off. Jake liked running at that big gray's side for whatever the reason, but when Thorne asked something of the dog, there was no hesitation in obeying. He stared after the retreating horse with a look of longing hanging in his green eyes.

Finding the young stranger's horse didn't take long. He had been right in figuring it had not gone

13

far. A horse with its reins dragging usually doesn't do much more than wander, and this one had managed to get the reins tangled in some low brush. Skittish when Thorne first came up, it quieted quickly when he stepped down from his gray and started talking to it while untangling the knotted reins. He ran a hand over the horse's red-brown flank, and then down each white stockinged leg. The horse was sound, but day-old sweat was matted into his hair, and he looked to have gone without water for about the same time. Being tangled in the brush like he'd been kept him from reaching the stream. Thorne gathered up the reins, and mounted, leading the horse to the stream. While the horse drank its fill, Thorne gazed about, always checking, examining, and cataloging in his mind. Shadows were lengthening throughout the valley. It was coming on to dark. Giving a gentle pull on the lines of the horse, Thorne was about to start back to camp when he saw a hoofprint in the soft earth along the streambank. He stepped down out of the saddle and got himself a closer look. That print could not have been more than a couple hours old, and it had not been made by either of Thorne's horses or the one he had just collected from the brush. This print showed a cracked shoe, and there were other prints leading off to the west. They were sunk deep in the soft earth, showing that the horse with the cracked shoe was packing a pretty good load. Just as sure as he was standing there, Thorne knew those tracks meant trouble. He muttered a few words that fitted his mood, and strode back to his patiently waiting gray. He had best get on back to camp pronto was his way of figuring it. There was no telling what kind of trouble he had stepped into without having a talk with that kid he had dug the bullet out of.

Stepping into the saddle, he headed the horse back to camp at a gallop.

CHAPTER TWO

The day had seemed longer than usual to Thorne by the time he got back into camp. There was a cool wind kicking up in the surrounding mountains and washing down over his valley. The sun was settling down behind the western mountains, throwing up the last brilliant rays of daylight. He rode in, picketed the horses, and stripped the saddles from their backs before he took himself a look in the young stranger's direction.

Jake was still lying there in the grass where he had dropped to stand watch when Thorne left. His massive head was still resting on his forepaws, but his solemn green eyes rested on the wounded man he had been left to watch, and every inch of him was alert. Without saying a word, Thorne got up a small fire and put some coffee on. That young boy glared at Jake and then at Thorne, but didn't seem to have anything to say right then.

"All right, Jake." Thorne dismissed the dog with a few quiet words and he disappeared down toward the stream. Thorne glanced after him. He knew Jake's habits well. First, the big dog would head for the stream for a drink of the cold water, then go out and hunt. Later, he would slip into camp quiet as a cat and sleep by Thorne's side. The dog always hunted his own food even though Thorne fed him. He never discouraged the dog's wanting to be independent. The way he lived, if anything happened to him, at least he wouldn't have to wonder what would happen to Jake. He'd take care of himself, one way or another.

"Reckon you could use something to eat by now," Thorne threw the words at the wounded man as he dug in his supplies for some beans and bacon. "You got lucky, boy." Thorne brought out the slug he had dug out of the other man's leg and tossed it to him. "Wouldn't have been much longer 'til you bled yourself dry."

Not looking exactly grateful, the younger man caught the bullet. "Where's my gun?" he demanded. "And don't call me boy," he added as an afterthought. "The name is Scott, Scott Mitchell." Stormy brown eyes rested on Thorne for an instant before they went wandering off again, trying to keep every direction in his sight at once. "You're so damned eager to save somebody's bacon, seems to me you could have left my gun."

Thorne chuckled. "Could've, but I worry about my own skin first. You might have just up and shot me when I rode up. You didn't have no call to worry none. A man couldn't set up for a long shot through these trees, and Jake wouldn't have let anybody get close enough for much else." He slid the bacon around in the pan. "Reckon you were safe enough." Thorne looked up. "Spotted some fresh tracks upstream a ways. Made by a big horse with a cracked shoe, and it looked to me like he was packing a pretty good load to boot." Thorne handed him a plate of grub and shook his head. "You really bought it, Scott. Whoever it is out there is sure enough dogging you."

"Ain't none of your affair, stranger." Scott belligerently took the offered food. "'Sides, I can take care of myself, just give me back my gun."

Thorne gazed at Scott from cool blue-gray eyes.

16

The sun had faded quickly, leaving them surrounded by the black coolness of the night. The small campfire flickered behind them. Thorne never had been known for being long on patience. Jake came from out of the shadows and dropped beside his master.

"I've got trouble of my own, Scott," Thorne said shortly, "and I sure ain't looking for a piece of yours. Trouble is, it's already here...you brought it with you and dumped it on my back steps. I'm settling in this valley so I'm gonna tell you straight out, I ain't about to stick my neck out for some fool kid who won't even tell me what the hell's going on." His blue-gray eyes were cold and hard. "I'm gonna give you a choice," he went on, not bothering to hide the anger in his deep voice. "I'll pile you in that saddle of yours and you can ride on out of this valley now, or you can stay here a few days to let that leg start to mending. If you figure to stay, you're gonna tell me why that fella out there is looking to blow out your lamp."

Scott glanced at his injured leg and glared at Thorne. His eyes held an anger that wasn't much different from Thorne's a few years back. "Who are you anyhow, mister?" Scott asked around a mouthful of beans.

"The name's Stevens," Thorne said flatly, "Thorne Stevens."

Looking up abruptly, Scott nodded. "I've heard the name." He set his empty plate aside. "A man'd be a fool to leave camp with a leg like this." He didn't feel any friendlier toward Thorne, but he sure enough wasn't any pilgrim. He knew what it would mean for him to start out of the valley with a bum leg and that gunman on his back. He wouldn't make it halfway up to that trail out. Scott was a rancher's

17

son, not a gunman, though he liked to think he could take care of himself, and he wanted others to think the same way. Scott didn't quite trust this stranger, but then he didn't really trust anyone else he could think of either. He was wary, and skittish as all get out, but if this man was the same Thorne Stevens he had heard about, he would be a hundred times safer in his camp than out riding through the night hoping to reach home before that gunslick put a slug in his back. If this here was the same Thorne Stevens who mopped up the countryside with the Barton gang down near the Mexican border, he had a reputation of being part tracker, part warrior, and part silver-tip grizzly with a sore paw.

"Ain't much to tell," Scott said at last. "You just waltzed yourself into the beginning of a range war. And the ones who got it started, they aren't going to take kindly to your helping me." He grinned without humor. "If you're fixing to stay in this valley, you're going to have to fight Harper Manning with the rest of us."

"I'm staying," Thorne stated flatly. "I hold what's mine," he said plain enough, and there was no bravado in his voice, only the calm statement of fact.

Scott couldn't help staring at him across the campfire. There was a feeling about the man who sat across from him, a feeling of power and a long-burning pent-up rage. Scott was even surprised to find himself talking to him. Any other man, and Scott would have told him to go to hell. He would have climbed back up on his horse, no matter what the consequences. There was something about Thorne Stevens that made him want to back up, sit down, and give the matter more consideration. That, Scott decided, was a man to ride the river with. And that wasn't something he had ever thought about any man, including his pa. That didn't mean his pa was not a strong man, even a ruthless man at times, but there was a different quality about Thorne, almost like a caged mountain cat, pacing, just waiting to get loose.

Thorne was careful to keep from staring into the flames of the campfire. He knew that bushwhacker out there, whoever he was, wouldn't be far from their camp. When he got around to moving in close Jake would pick up his scent. When that happened, Thorne wasn't going to be night blind because he got careless. He glanced at Jake. The big dog was alert, but quiet.

"You know who that fella is out there?" Thorne asked at last.

"Just that he's one of Manning's men," Scott said with a shrug. "It doesn't matter which one."

"Sure as hell does, boy." Thorne let the boy slip out in his speech and silently cursed himself for it, but kept on with what he had started to say. "If I knew that hombre, I'd know what to expect. If you knew him, you could tell me what to expect. The way things are, Jake is gonna have to let me know when something out there changes, but he can't spell it out in words."

Scott shrugged. "Still don't know any more than I already told you."

It was beginning to look to Thorne like things might have been considerably easier if he'd just left Scott Mitchell up on the side of that mountain with his gun and his own trouble to keep him company. His breath sort of oozed out in a long, controlled sigh as he handed Scott his gun. Thorne remembered a few years back...circumstances had been different, but he hadn't been any better off

19

than Scott. Backing into a corner to fight the rest of the world like a wounded bear. He had done his share of snapping and snarling, and when the dust had settled, it sure hadn't gotten him very far.

Thorne remembered what had started it for him. He had had a good enough life back in Missouri until he was fifteen. That was when his pa died of the fever. His ma had been dead for five years. First thing them good folks did was separate him and his little brother, Zeke. Zeke hadn't been quite nine years old then. They gave Zeke to some wagon-trail folks who claimed they couldn't take Thorne too. They had been heading west and Thorne hadn't seen hide nor hair of Zeke since. To top it off, the bank stepped in and took his pa's little farm saying it was for money owed. Thorne had been left alone with nothing. His pa never had been too friendly to folks, and they weren't none too friendly toward Thorne. He had taken to drifting and made out all right, but it was a painful memory, and it had not given him much cause to be figuring all men for brothers.

"How'd you come to get this far?" Thorne asked, shaking loose from old thoughts. "This valley is a pretty far piece from most anything else in these parts."

"I didn't see him," Scott answered, "but I reckon the gunman trailed me. I had me a run in with some of Manning's men when they said I was trespassing when I crossed onto his range to get back a couple head of our beef. Manning's crew is a gun-happy bunch, so I lit out. They had me cut off from my pa's place and I didn't figure too many folks knew about this place. I planned to camp out here for a couple of days, then slip around them and back to the ranch. That gunslick fella got a slug into me when I was coming down off the trail." Scott

20

gingerly rubbed his sore leg. "Beats me how I lost him."

Thorne checked his guns and snuffed out the campfire, then got ahold of Scott under his arms and dragged him back several feet away from where the camp had been. Scott kept his mouth shut though he didn't take kindly to being moved without being asked. Then Thorne took the horses' picket pins and moved them deep into the trees behind where he had left Scott. He hoped to make it look like they had cleared out fast, and bring that gunman in to them. He had done it more than once in the past. He had hired his gun out himself a time or two long ago, though he wasn't proud of it. A man didn't live the way Thorne had without having drygulchers on his tail.

"Keep the gun handy," Thorne told Scott, "and sleep light. Sometimes this trick works, but there've been times when it hasn't."

Scott didn't have to ask what Thorne was talking about. All he had to do was take himself a good look. Thorne was drawing that gunslick right into their camp. Most times a man with a gun, hunting another, would not be able to resist investigating if he saw a campfire disappear from view as theirs had. Deep down, Scott was not sure that bringing that gunslinger down on them was what he wanted. He was not one to back down from a fight, but he wasn't too eager to bring one on either. The men working for Harper Manning were far out of his league and he knew it. Scott glanced from the gun he held in his hand to Thorne. He was running this show. There was a quiet confidence about Thorne, and Scott wished he shared it.

Night dragged past. The moon set, and it could not have been much more than an hour until dawn.

21

Thorne was beginning to wonder it the gunman was going to show at all when Jake growled deep in his chest. His massive head came up and he stared into the darkness, ears pricked forward. He growled again, so low in his chest that Thorne could feel the dog's warm body vibrating up against him, like the purring of a great cat. His Colt in his hand, Thorne remained pressed up against the trunk of a tree and touched Jake's head to warn him to silence. The cold night air washed over Thorne like a flowing stream, to bring with it the soft sounds of the night. A stream chuckled softly in its bed not more than fifty yards away. Soft, night winds whispered quietly through the branches high overhead, and far off in the distance was the mournful howl of wolves on the move. Dead leaves carpeting the ground rustled as a breath of air stirred them from their resting places. Thorne heard all those sounds, and more, but the sounds he was waiting to hear wouldn't fit in with the rest. Whoever was out there was good, better than most, but he hadn't counted on Jake's hearing, or Thorne's alertness. Scott was inexperienced and wounded as well. Odds were that he would have slept until it was too late. Thorne flipped a stone in his direction to wake him. There were times when he wondered how anybody lived long enough to get old.

Scott came awake with a start as the stone found its mark, and the sounds Thorne had been waiting for came at the same instant. The leaves rustled, but now there was an uneven rhythm to them, like footsteps. A twig snapped nearby and in the quiet of the night it seemed loud enough to bring a bear out of his winter's sleep. Jake's lips curled back from gleaming white teeth in a silent snarl. As always, the big dog could feel the tension in Thorne. Ghostlike,

22

Jake came to his feet and slipped off between the trees to scout the man as he approached. Thorne watched him go, knowing the dog knew what he was doing. Many times before, Jake had been through situations like this. Thorne glanced over at Scott. He wished he could say the same for him. When it came to gun trouble, that boy was as green as the grass of Kentucky. He wouldn't admit it, but it was written all over him. He didn't come awake all at once as a man would who had lived for some time under nothing but the sky. His movements weren't even, they were fast and jerking, the kind that drew attention and gun muzzles.

Loud and menacing, Jake's distinct growl sounded from not more than a few feet to Thorne's left, and he spotted the dark outline of a man framed in the darkness of the predawn. The footsteps froze, and Thorne could see Jake's green eyes glowing beyond the dark outline of the man.

Thorne was lying belly down beside the massive trunk of the old tree, and he figured he had that gunman up about as close as he was going to let him get.

"That's far enough." Thorne's deep voice cut through the night air plain and clear. "Drop the gun and step back easy." There was only a fifty-fifty chance the man would do as he was told. Thorne wasn't kidding himself, he had come across men before who would rather give up their lives than their guns, and facing him, they usually did.

For a few seconds, though, Thorne thought this one was going to show more good sense and a little less pride, but he was wrong. That gunman must have believed the fact that it was so dark would give him the edge he needed against a drawn gun cause all of a sudden he brought that gun of his up and

23

fired. The slug tore into the tree where Thorne lay, throwing dust and splinters into his face, but not doing any damage. As Thorn rolled over once and squeezed off his shot he heard Scott's gun explode a little behind him. That dark, man-shape stumbled backwards, crashing into some low brush, and lay still. Bristling and growling low as he circled the body, Jake came up beside the fallen man, seeming to want to make sure the matter had been taken care of proper.

Thorne came easily to his feet and crossed to where the man lay. He didn't plan on finding the man alive, and he was right. Jamming his gun back into his holster he quieted Jake with a few low words. He rested his hands on his belt and cursed silently to himself. Thorne had come all the way across the country just to keep from having to do again what he had just done. He glanced back at Scott and sighed. It was true, he had drawn the gunman in, but it had been either that or let him attack on his own ground, and Thorne had never been one to give an enemy equal footing if it could be avoided. That didn't change none the way he felt. He had hoped he would never have to kill another human being and he couldn't get through even one night in his new beginning, far from any town without a killing. Thorne had felt sick inside for a good while of all the killing, but it didn't look to him like trouble was ever going to stop being brought to him.

Already the eastern sky was brightening and the first sliver of sunlight broke through the gloom. Thorne wheeled abruptly on his heel and started back to camp for a shovel and the pack horse. Moving the body was easier than to pack up and move the camp and he wasn't about to have a grave in camp. With the danger past, Jake was once more relaxed and moved easily at his side.

"He dead?" Scott asked as Thorne came up.

Thorne nodded. "About as dead as they come." He dug a shovel out of his pack and took the pack horse off his picket pin. Thorne ran a hand through his shaggy brown hair. "I'll be gone a spell," he said offhand. "Come on, Jake," he said over his shoulder to the dog.

With hardly a pause, Thorne loaded the dead man onto the horse's back and started out across the tall grasses to find a gravesite in some hidden hollow. The sun was creeping above the eastern horizon, sending an almost imperceptible warmth flooding across the valley. Jake loped on ahead, and Thorne kept on walking, leading the horse. His was a grim chore, and he would just as soon have it over with.

CHAPTER THREE

Coming down out of the mountains was something Thorne hadn't figured on doing until spring. But with Scott Mitchell on his hands, there wasn't any choice. He sure wasn't spending the winter snowbound in that valley with an inexperienced and arrogant kid. The thing to do was get him back to his pa and let him have the worries, and Thorne was sure Scott gave him a passel of them.

A couple of days of hobbling around on that bum leg was all Thorne figured Scott needed to be strong enough to travel, so he piled him in his saddle and started on back along the trail down. The pack horse he left behind, grazing on the valley's thick green grass. There would be no reason for him to wander very far, and Thorne did not need the animal along for supplies. If this country was anywhere near as rough as Scott had been telling him, he didn't need anything else to keep an eye on. Jake trotted easily at the big gray's side. There was nothing to worry about there. The big dog could take care of himself...probably better even than Thorne could.

The trip back was not going to be any picnic for Scott with that bad leg, but Thorne couldn't afford to put off the trip, no knowing for sure when the snowfall would come that would cut off the valley for the winter. In these parts it was always a guessing game. A big storm could come tomorrow, or not for several weeks. It depended on the whims of nature.

Leaving the valley, the trail was easy as it always was unless there was ice on the rocky ledge. There was a distinct chill to the air in spite of the bright morning sun. The bite of winter was in the air, and Thorne knew well that the soft, wafting breezes that washed over a man like the scent of a woman's perfume wouldn't fill the air again until spring. He led the way until they reached the end of the narrow mountain trail and few words passed between himself and Scott. Jake loped on a little ahead, always scouting, as Scott drew his horse up alongside Thorne's where the trail began to widen. Favoring his still sore right leg, Scott rode a little off balance but Thorne had to admit that he was a right spunky kid.

The narrow, rocky trail had turned back into open meadows and stands of tall trees. Thorne looked slowly around. It would not be long until that snow fell, and he was determined to be back within the sheltering circle of mountains that bordered his

26

valley before it fell.

"My pa's spread ain't a far piece from here," Scott broke into Thorne's thoughts. 'We should get there well before sunset."

Thorne nodded slowly, his gaze continuing to wander. Somebody was up ahead in the cover of some trees. Jake was acting a bit edgy, and those trees were the only cover for quite a stretch. Thorne edged his horse closer to Scott's, forcing him to veer off more to the east. If there were men inside the fringe of trees, it was plain they didn't want to be seen, and all that meant to Thorne was trouble. If he could, he would just as soon steer clear of it. Plumb tired and worn to the bone, it seemed to Thorne he was always worrying about other folks troubles. He had been alone ever since he was fifteen, no family to worry about, or to worry about him. But it seemed like life was bound and determined to have him looking out for someone. Now it was this Mitchell kid. Thorne knew if he had any brains he would leave Scott now and head out before trouble had a chance to start. He would have done it too, if he didn't have a conscience, and if he had not seen what happened in areas where there had been other range wars. He decided he had gotten himself mixed up in this when he helped Scott back there in the valley, and he wouldn't be shut of it until he left Scott with his pa.

"What the hell you doing?" Scott demanded angrily of Thorne. "I told you Pa's place was due south, right through them trees." Scott didn't understand this strangely quiet man...a man who never told him anything. It was damn hard to get friendly with him. Still, Scott respected him, even managed a grudging liking for the stranger.

Giving Scott a sharp glance from cool blue-gray

27

eyes Thorne wondered how this kid would ever survive a range war. "Whose range are we on right now, Scott?" He appraised Scott closely. He wasn't any kid by this country's standards, but it was hard to think of him as anything else. There was just something about him.

"Harper Manning's," Scott said quickly, "but I don't see how we're gonna get off it any faster this way."

Thorne nodded in the direction of the trees. "Some of your friends must have seen us coming. Probably fixing to give you a real proper welcome."

Scott jerked around and looked toward the clump of trees. "I don't see anything," Scott said quickly. He glanced back at Thorne, his brown eyes holding a mixture of doubt and puzzlement, but, at the same time, he was remembering this man's reputation. Thorne would be right, Scott was sure of it, but he didn't see anything. Alone, he would have ridden right on through.

"Jake didn't need to see anything," Thorne said, his voice conversational, like there was nothing more important on his mind than a pleasant day, and a nice ride. "He smelled it and heard it, and he reads trouble real good."

Glancing down at the huge, brute of a dog, Scott could see Jake's ears moving constantly, and his sensitive nose testing the air. The dog's head turned continually toward the trees, ears pricked, and his nose sampling the wind.

"When they come," Scott heard Thorne saying, "keep your hand clear of your gun. If there's any shooting to be done, let them start it."

Scott's mouth felt dry, like it was lined with cotton. He had always fancied himself as pretty good with a gun, but he had never shot at anything

28

more than a few rabbits for the table, or some fast-moving Indians that he never really got a good look at. By any standards, he wouldn't be considered fast on the draw, and the thought of a stand up shoot out, face to face, tied a knot in his stomach. But Thorne had said it so easy, as if he did it every day. Well, Scott reflected, didn't he?

"Why don't we make a run for it?" Scott suggested. "Avoid any shooting." He hoped he sounded like he wasn't hunting trouble instead of like he was just plain scared.

Thorne shook his head. "The way you've been riding, that horse of yours would dump you before we could get a hundred yards." He could sense Scott's uneasiness, and the sound of hoofbeats was coming up fast behind them. There wasn't anything he could do but hope Scott would carry his weight. If there was shooting, that would take a lot of sand.

As the hoofbeats came closer, Thorne wheeled his horse to face them. Scott followed his example, uncertainly watching the approach of the riders. Instinctively, Jake moved off several yards to one side, the hairs on the back of his neck bristling. Having them turn around to face them instead of running was something the oncoming riders hadn't figured on. Folks in these parts usually ran like the devil was on their trail when they spotted some of Harper Manning's men coming over a rise. They slowed their horses to a brisk trot as they covered the last few strides and pulled up in front of them.

Thorne's tanned and weathered face was expressionless. When he spoke there was an icy note in his voice. "You boys looking for something?" he asked quietly of the four riders facing them.

All four were gun hands, Thorne had seen men of their cut enough times in the past to know what it was he was looking at. An aura of self-confidence surrounded them and three had half grins on their faces. One had a long face that looked like a horse with his forelock hanging in his face. Another was thin as a rail and looked like he was strung tight as barbed wire. The third appeared youngest, but there was authority in his manner. Whether it was deserved or only tolerated by the others was a question worth wondering about. The fourth was hanging back a bit and eyeing Thorne closer than any of the other three. There was something familiar about that man, something that wasn't good. Something told Thorne he had best put his finger on it before he got into a tangle with him. He was some older than the other three gunmen with him, and it was plain he had managed to stay alive by playing hunches and knowing what he was getting himself into before he got in too deep to get himself back out.

Thorne sat the big gray quiet, his big, squared hands resting easily on the saddle horn, but his heavy green jacket was pushed back behind his holster, leaving the butt of his Colt exposed to an easy grab if he needed it. Jake was standing a little to one side, snarling and generally not letting anybody forget he was handy. A couple of the gunmen looked a mite uneasily in the big dog's direction. A dog that looked like a wolf, and was bigger than a half-grown catamount was an even better equalizer than a gun with some men. They would sooner risk a bullet than those teeth. Jake never had been that friendly with folks other than Thorne anyway, and these past couple of days had made him more edgy than usual.

One of the riders, a man with snake eyes, a stringy black mustache, and a mouth that looked

30

like he had sucked too many lemons at a young age, spoke up, figuring himself to be the man to be reckoned with. "You're trespassing," he said bluntly but with a false note of humor in his voice. "You've got Mitchell's kid with you. He knows you're both trespassing."

"Passing through," Thorne said easily. "Don't even figure to water our horses."

Snake Eyes flicked his glance back and forth between Thorne and Scott. He'd seen the Mitchell kid before. It would not take much to be done with him. The stranger with him was another matter. He was so quiet, so ready. There was no scare in him, no back up. It was clear to him he would not be as easy to handle as some of the ranchers in these parts. Still, he was only one man.

"I know how it is," Snake Eyes said, trying to sound genuinely concerned, "but we're hired to keep folks off'a Mister Manning's range, and we got our job to do."

Suddenly, the older man from the back of the little group urged his horse forward, coming up alongside Snake Eyes. "That there's Thorne Stevens." His voice was urgent, low and harsh.

Snake Eyes turned sharply on the older man. "Don't give a damn who it is." His eyes snapped, and in that instant the other two men with him went for their guns, their hands barely reaching their holsters on the downswing before they froze. Not slow on reaction time himself, Snake Eyes spun back around to find the muzzle of Thorne's gun covering them. It was as if the gun had materialized there out of thin air.

Thorne had been waiting for some distraction to give him the instant that he needed when attention would be drawn away from himself and Scott. That

31

man recognizing him had done it, and his Colt Peacemaker had come into his hand as naturally as his next breath. Scott stared at him a few seconds. He had been watching, and he hadn't even seen it when Thorne had actually drawn. Finally, he pulled his own gun from his holster, though he didn't reckon Thorne needed any help.

The air was filled with tension, but the expression on Thorne's face didn't change, except for the deepening of some lines around his eyes. He had learned long ago that a man who wanted to keep his hide whole didn't let other folks know what was going on inside. Thorne knew the kind of man Snake Eyes was and there was just enough of the wild animal left in Thorne to just as soon shoot him down like a rabid dog. Logic told him that if he did not, others would die at the hand of that man before he was stopped. Thorne never had been a cold-blooded killer.

He could be ruthless when a situation demanded it, but this one didn't. There were times, he thought, when life might have been a whole lot easier if he had been.

"Drop your guns and climb down off'a your horses." Thorne's voice was low but it carried loud enough to be heard. "Now," he added pointedly when Snake Eyes hesitated, considering reaching for his gun instead of dropping it to the dirt. Thorne fastened his gaze on one man after another as they dropped their guns and stepped down from the saddle. He would remember each face. Thorne knew he would have to. There could come a time when his life would depend on his remembering who they were. Hired guns were not known as a forgiving breed.

"Scott," Thorne said without taking his gaze from

32

the four men standing on the ground in front of him, "get down, and get their guns and horses...I'll keep you covered."

Scott did as Thorne said, gathering the guns and the reins of the four horses, then managing to climb back up into the saddle with that bad leg even though the sweat broke out across his forehead as if he had been doused with a bucket of water.

"Head for those trees," Thorne told Scott when he was again on his horse.

Scott was getting so used to following the orders that Thorne gave in such a quiet, authoritative voice that he just naturally took out for the trees, leading the horses, without question.

Having Scott search the gunmen for hideout guns was something Thorne hadn't wanted to risk. One wrong move, and they could have had a real shooting war on their hands mighty quick. Thorne had been up the creek a few times, and he knew all about hideout guns. Fact of the matter was, he'd used one himself a time or two although he was not packing one now. Hideout guns had a mighty short range so the trick was to get out of range before turning his back.

"We'll leave your horses somewhere beyond those trees," Thorne said mildly. He glanced down at the big dog standing a few feet away. "Let's move out, Jake," he said, backing his big gray a few strides before wheeling him and lighting out on the run after Scott.

The big gray moved smoothly and Jake moved up, running a little ahead of the horse. No shots came from behind, so Thorne figured that old Snake Eyes back there just didn't want to waste a shot from that little gun Thorne was sure he had. He caught up with Scott just before he reached the trees

33

and reined in the gray to match the stride of Scott's mount. They weren't throwing up much dust as they moved, the ground was hard, and the rhythmic beating of the horses' hoofs thudded softly against their ears. Thorne glanced over his shoulder once. All four gunmen were standing where he had left them. Soon they'd be starting to walk, and by the time they found their horses and guns they would be plenty tired, and mad enough to be pawing the ground with blood in their eyes. Thorne sighed. Seemed like folks was always hunting trouble. Now he would have some of his own to tangle with. There would be trouble next time he crossed trails with any one of that brunch and he knew it. But the one he figured on keeping a wary eye out for was Snake Eyes. Thorne had taken his measure, and that one was a prime back shooter, if he had ever laid eyes on one.

CHAPTER FOUR

Scott did not have a whole lot to say when Thorne caught up with him just east of them trees so they continued on in silence. They left the horses belonging to the gunman picketed on the far side of the trees before moving on south onto range owned by Scott's pa. The country did not change much as they rode. It was rolling land, thick with grass browning before winter's onslaught. There were open meadows, abundant streams, and, in the distance, lofty peaks capped with snow. Some gray clouds were hanging around the peaks to the north, but Thorne didn't figure they were brewing up a storm. A little snow tonight with most of it pretty

34

well blowing off tomorrow was the way he saw it. It wouldn't be too much longer though before a full-blown norther came through, and Thorne was thinking of all the things he hadn't done in his valley to be ready. It appeared to him that he was going to have to lay low and work whenever the weather broke. He should have arrived in the spring, but that was too late to change now. There was quite a chill in the air. Thorne had little doubt that there would be some snow before he managed to get back to the valley.

"Ranchhouse is right on the other side of those trees," Scott said cheerfully as they rode up a hollow, jarring Thorne from his thoughts.

Thorne's jacket was still hooked around behind his holster. A man couldn't be too careful, to his way of thinking, in country that was splitting apart with a range war. He had long ago given up figuring any place as safe. Thorne had a liking for Scott, but had to admit he wouldn't be unhappy to be shut of him and clear out of the area before anything else could happen.

Jake loped on up ahead as they came in sight of the ranchhouse nestling on the lower slope of a hill. His nose to the wind as usual, the big dog had his ears pricked forward, and they were moving continuously from side to side. He paused, gave a short bark, then moved on ahead.

"Someone's up ahead," Thorne was keeping an eye on Jake. There wasn't much the dog missed.

"Probably Pa," Scott assumed. "Reckon he figures me for dead by now."

Riding on the inside as they were passing by the trees on the way up to the house, Thorne had decided Scott was probably right when a rifle cracked off to his right, and the bullet threw up dirt

35

in front of his gray.

"That's far enough," a voice snapped from the cover of the trees. The voice was sharp, commanding, and it belonged to a woman.

Reining in the gray sharply, Thorne glanced around, unable to pinpoint where the voice had come from. He didn't rightly know what he was going to do, since a woman had never pulled a rifle on him before, but he felt as if he should at least know where she was. Jake was eager to head on into the trees, but Thorne stopped him with a word.

Looking to be more angry than worried, Scott urged his horse forward until he could see and be seen past Thorne. "Brandy, put that thing down and climb on out of there."

There was a long pause, then the voice came again, this time questioning. "Scott?"

"Who does it look like?" Scott's voice was exasperated.

There was some rustling and a shaking of some limbs up in the trees, then a small, slender figure appeared at the trunk of one of the larger trees and ran in their direction. Thorne relaxed when he realized Scott knew whoever it was with that rifle and let his hands rest quietly on his saddle horn as she came toward them. There wasn't much to her really. She was small and slender, holding herself very straight and moving with a long, swinging gait until she was only a couple of yards away. "Scott!" she said breathlessly. "We thought you were dead!" For all the attention he got, Thorne could have been a hitching post but he could see that her gun was ready. "When you didn't come back I didn't know what to do." Any man could see she wanted to run to him and throw her arms around him, but she stayed where she was. Her face was flushed from the

36

run in the cold air, her brown eyes bright and shining, and her raven-black hair hanging in loose disarray down to the middle of her back. She had eyebrows that were black as midnight against soft white skin and they were shaped as delicately as a pair of bird's wings. Her small nose was upturned on the end and there was a suggestion of freckles, once bright and prominent, now only a deepening of the skin tone. She was wearing a boy's jeans, boots, and a heavy fringed leather jacket. The jacket and blue shirt underneath were open at the neck, revealing a long, slender white throat.

With outthrust chin, she stood there in front of them, her rifle still trained on Thorne. To Thorne, she looked like some wild, free young animal, challenging intruders and defending her territory. Tousled, wind-blown hair fell heavily about her shoulders, forming a frame for her fine features.

"Well," she said at last, looking toward Thorne, "he looked to me like something Harper Manning might dig up."

Thorne looked over toward Scott for an explanation, and Scott just sighed. "This is my sister, Brandy," he explained to Thorne, then turned back to his sister who was still standing a little ways off, and holding that rifle like she knew how to use it. "Aw, come on, Brandy," Scott protested, "if he was one of Manning's men I'd be dead and buried out there somewheres, and you know it."

Brandy's brown eyes flashed. "Now how would I know that? Might be this fella here had something else on his mind, like how he could get all the way out here without getting himself shot."

"Well, then I'm telling ya, Brandy, his name is Thorne Stevens and he saved my life. Put that thing down." Scott's anger was getting plenty hot.

37

Brandy stared up into Thorne's quiet, passive face for long seconds, her deep brown eyes frankly appraising.

"We better get back to the house," she finally said. "Pa will be awful glad to see you." She made a move toward Scott's horse to ride double, but he side-stepped his mount away from her.

Scott grinned a mite. "Got my leg tore up pretty good. I don't want you banging it around, so if you want to ride, climb up behind Thorne."

Brandy made a point of handing Scott her rifle, then stepped up beside Thorne's big gray. Thorne kicked his left foot free of the stirrup and reached a hand down to help her up. It was like laying hold of a wraith, and she swung up behind him light as a feather. He felt her arms circle his waist, strong arms, but unmistakably a woman's. Thorne had to admit there was something about her that attracted him almost from the first moment he saw her. Could be it was the wildness. The look about her that said she could take on this brutal, wild country, and have the strength to win, when most women would fall apart or just plain give up.

Almost before Thorne's horse came to a complete halt, Brandy slid from his back and darted inside the house. Being careful of that bad leg of his, Scott stepped down and looped his reins over the hitching post in front of the house.

"Climb down," Scott said. "Pa's going to want to meet the man settling that valley. He had his eye on it a couple of times himself."

Thorne glanced at the sun. It was getting late. He was itching to get started back, but a few more minutes couldn't make much difference. It would be dark long before he got back to the valley anyway.

He swung down from the gray's back, looping the

38

reins over the hitching post as the front door to the house opened and Brandy reappeared with an older man at her side who Thorne figured to be their pa. The short, middle-aged man crossed the porch with a rolling gait on bow-legs to embrace his son and clap him soundly on the back. For long seconds there was silence and Thorne could feel the emotion in the air. Then the older man turned to Thorne.

"The name's Angus Mitchell," he said quickly, thrusting out his hand. Thorne could see the mist in his bright black eyes even though he was trying hard to hide it. "I want you to know that I'm beholden to you for what you did for Scott."

The handshake of Angus Mitchell was firm and dry, though not intended to test another man's strength as some did. Thorne looked into the other man's tanned and weathered face with its short, wiry black beard flecked with gray, the long, straight, almost aristocratic nose and the black eyes, hard as crystal and black as coal. Having folks figure they were beholden to him wasn't something Thorne was used to. It sort of left him tongue-tied, and feeling like a kid caught playing hooky from school.

"You'll be staying the night." Angus made the statement as a fact, not a question.

Thorne started to protest, but Angus held up his hand. "I don't know the whole of what happened, but I'll not have a man who saved my son's life leave this house without at least a good meal to fill his belly." His eyes were bright with good humor. "And," he added, "by the time we finish eating, it won't be fit for man nor beast out there among Manning's back-shooting buzzards."

A slow smile spread across Thorne's face. It would be nice to be around Brandy a bit longer. He wondered if she could cook. Brandy smiled at

39

Thorne from the doorway almost like she could read his mind, and went on back inside the house.

"All right," Thorne finally agreed. "But I'll be pulling out before dawn."

Angus shrugged. "I'll take what I can get."

The men went into the house with Jake following closely at their heels. Angus took special care to make the animal as welcome in his home as Thorne. The big dog moved off to one side and stretched out on a rug near the fireplace, a luxury he didn't very often receive. Scott dropped into an overstuffed chair and propped up his injured leg, letting out a long sigh.

"That's quite a sister you've got," Thorne said with admiration to Scott while his pa brought in the drinking whiskey.

"She's a wildcat, and half the territory knows it," Scott chuckled.

Angus poured the drinks and glared at his son. "I've told you before not to talk about your sister like that. You're old enough to have better sense. I thought I taught you some respect for womenfolk."

Scott started to say something, but Brandy cut him off. "It's all right, Pa." She came off the stairway with a swirl of heavy skirts and gave her brother a cool smile. "The next time Scott gets himself pinned under his horse in a mudhole and the mud starts to oozing up around his chin I'll remember it's not ladylike for me to wade in and help him. I'll just naturally trot my buggy on down the road for help," she said cuttingly. "With a little luck, I might even get back before he drowns."

Brandy was good and mad; Scott knew all the signs. He couldn't even remember ever seeing her in a buggy! She had ridden astraddle ever since they had been kids. "Aw, come on, Brandy," Scott said

40

sheepishly, "you know I was just funnin'."

Thorne shook his head. Seemed like brothers and sisters just naturally had to pick at each other. He watched Brandy cross the room, a picture of dignity and reserve. That Scott had a powerful lot of learning to do where his sister was concerned. Just like her pa said, she was a woman all right. It looked to Thorne that Scott was so busy just growing up with her that he didn't notice when the change came. He was still thinking of her as his little sister.

She had her long black hair brushed smoothly back, but it still hung free, with only a ribbon to hold it back. Her eyes were bright, and a shy smile slipped past her cool reserve, dimpling her cheeks.

"Dinner's almost ready," she said lightly.

Gallantly, Thorne offered her his arm and walked her to the dining room. Scott stared in open-mouthed surprise, and Angus just smiled. He knew his daughter. It wasn't often that she was interested in a man, but it was plain to him that this was one of those times. Living way out here the way they did, it was not often that Brandy even got to talk to another man other than her pa, Scott, and maybe some hired cowpuncher.

At dinner the talk turned to the problem that was facing the ranchers, and it seemed like it could all be summed up in two words: Harper Manning. The name was a new one to Thorne. He had never heard it before except from Scott, but the way Angus Mitchell told it, he was bound and determined to wind up owning half of the Wyoming Territory. If Wyoming became a state soon, as most folks were figuring, Mr. Manning would wind up being one powerful man. There was even talk that he might be heading to be governor of the new state. Seemed like the two things Harper Manning wanted most

41

out of life were land and power. He had made it plain that he had decided having the first would get him the second. Thorne had been around in different places during a couple of other range wars. What came with them wasn't pretty. People died, and most times it was the wrong people. Thorne had ridden into this, and he was going to be plumb happy to go and get himself snowed in that valley for the winter. The more he saw of folks, the more he figured it just didn't pay to deal with them unless a body had no choice.

Brandy cleared the table and disappeared into the kitchen to clean up. It had been a long spell since Thorne had sat down to a spread like she laid out on the table. Beef and potatoes with a thick gravy had been followed with bread that had to have been baked earlier that day, and something Thorne hadn't laid eyes on since he was a kid...baked apples. And after all the days he had spent on the trail, it didn't escape his attention that there was not a bean to be seen on that table.

After Brandy left the room, Angus gazed levelly into Thorne's eyes. "You better watch yourself, Harper Manning has a knife for everybody's back. There's been some crazy, fool talk about the railroad coming through here somewheres. I don't believe a word of it, but Harper, he takes it like gospel. And having people get in his way isn't something he takes kindly to. Even said he'd leave my place alone if I let him marry up with Brandy." Angus emptied his cup and grinned. "He seemed some upset when I told him to go to hell." With that last comment, he rose and gestured for his son and Thorne to join him back in the parlor for a couple of drinks.

As they came into the warm, cheerful room the first thing that caught Thorne's attention was the sight of Brandy bending over Jake to pet him.

"I wouldn't do that," Thorne said quickly, but he was already too late. Jake wasn't a dog to take kindly to folks and he had already taken a chunk out of one or two to prove it.

Brandy smiled slowly. Jake's tail moved back and forth across the floor to show he didn't mind as she stroked his silky head. He was doing more than just tolerating her touch, he was enjoying it. Thorne shook his head in puzzlement. It didn't seem like he would ever figure Jake out.

Rising, Brandy looked up full into Thorne's face. "Such a vicious dog," she prodded gently. Wrapping her shawl tightly about her shoulders she started for the door. "I was about to step outside for some fresh air, won't you join me?"

Angus poured himself and Scott a drink, pointedly leaving Thorne's glass empty. As though by invisible command, Jake jumped up from his scrap of rug by the fire and slipped outside between them.

Outside, the night air was stirring, carrying the chilly bite of winter. Stars blinked in the black night sky as the clouds gathered to blot them out. The big dog moved off into the shadows to investigate the interesting smells that drifted past his nose. They stood on the wooden porch gazing off across the open land that rolled away from their feet.

"Jake don't take to many," Thorne told Brandy quietly.

"I haven't found an animal yet that would bother me. Pa tells me my mother was the same way."

Thorne felt some awkward. It wasn't often that he talked to womenfolk, and when he did, it was usually to a saloon girl in some town where he would never see her again. The words never came

43

easy and slick to him like they did to some men, but there was something about Brandy that was working through the armor he'd built up over the years.

"You lived out here long?" Thorne asked.

Brandy laughed, the sound blending with the soft whisper of the night wind. "Born and raised. Don't tell me Pa wasn't carrying on in there about how I didn't belong way out here in the middle of nowhere?"

"Well," Thorne admitted with a grin, "seems to me I recall something 'bout that last part."

"Thought so," Brandy began, then abruptly turned her head gazing down toward the barn. "Did you hear something?"

Silence fell between them. "Sounds like a herd moving this way mighty fast," he said quietly. "I reckon you better get on into the house." If they were in the first few sparks of a wildfire range war in these parts, Thorne had reason to know what was coming. He had seen a herd of cattle used as a weapon before. There wasn't much that would stop them once they started to run. Any rancher knew as much.

Just as Thorne turned to open the door, the first shot cracked through the stillness of the night. Something hit him a powerful whack on the side of his head. Knees buckling, he had enough presence of mind to fling out an arm, catching Brandy about the waist and pulling her down as he fell. Another shot split the air, throwing up splinters behind where she'd been standing. The shot hadn't knocked Thorne cold and he shook his head against the roaring and pounding inside like an angry bull. Rolling to his knees, he clawed his Colt from his holster as he staggered to his feet. The distant pound of hoofs had grown to a roar and Thorne could see

44

the first bobbing heads surging over the distant rise. His own problem was nearer at hand. The shots that had come so dangerously close had come from the direction of the barn. Brandy stayed where she was, flat on the porch floorboards Showing a lot better sense than most, she didn't stand up and risk drawing fire in her direction. Scott showed himself in the window above Brandy as the third slug slapped into the porch post next to Thorne and he returned the fire.

A thin trickle of blood was running down the side of Thorne's head into his left eye. Steadying his gun with both hands, he snapped off a couple of shots toward the barn even though he didn't know exactly where the gunman was firing on them from.

Brandy's pa was at the door, easing it open slowly to reach his daughter. With a couple of long strides, Thorne was off the porch and slipping alongside the house, drawing the gunman's attention away from the porch while Angus dragged Brandy inside.

Hunkering down next to the corner of the house, Thorne, his eyes used to the darkness, looked for some sign of the gunman in the barn. His wound wasn't much more than a scratch, but it stung worse than the lash of a bullwhip, and the blood that trickled down the side of his face threw off his aim. He wiped the blood away from his eye with an irritated gesture.

The cattle were drawing closer, the pounding of their running hoofs blending together to sound like one continuous peel of thunder rolling down out of the mountains. From the sounds of it, Thorne didn't plan on too many, probably just whatever the raiders could round up on their way over to the Mitchell spread. This time, it seemed, the stampeding cattle would be mostly for cover while that gunman in the

45

barn and whoever else was coming along with the cattle would see how much damage they could do. Thorne was guessing at how long it would take the cattle to hit the main yard on the dead run when he saw a shadowy shape appear from the shadows at the side of the barn. He was crouched low between the side of the barn, and a buckboard left up against the corral.

Then, above the pounding of oncoming hoofs and the excited bellows of the cattle, Thorne heard Jake's full, piercing howl that meant he was closing in on something. And Thorne knew what that something was. Till then, he had forgotten that Jake had come out the door with him and Brandy. Jake was a fighter. Given reason, he would go after anything, and now he was after the gunman crouched by the barn.

With the cattle bearing down on them, the gunman slipped from the blackest shadows, still crouched low, heading for where he had left his horse on the far side of the barn. Thorne caught sight of him moving, and brought his Colt up when Jake appeared from out of nowhere. The big dog was in midstride and going straight for the shadowy form. Thorne held his fire. Something warned the crouched and running gunman. A sound, a movement, something caused him to turn. With all the power and drive of a big cat in his trail-hardened muscles, Jake left the ground in a leap that caught the gunman at almost head level with the force of a charging bull. The gun flew from his hand, and he slammed into the ground where he lay motionless. Snarling his anger, Jake stood stiff-legged to one side. Only a matter of seconds remained until those cattle hit, but Thorne lit out across that yard, grabbed the man under the arms and dragged him back up beside the barn, calling Jake to come with him.

Cattle surged into the ranch yard like water released from a broken dam. Thorne could see a couple of riders in the dim blackness but he didn't fire on them. Scott and his pa were already taking care of that from the house, and Thorne figured he was too much in the open to risk lead flying in his direction. The men running the cattle took a couple of shots in the direction of the house, but didn't hit much besides a couple of windows, then kept on riding into the night's covering darkness.

Thorne let his breath out in a long sigh. This had been the beginning all right. This one wasn't much more than a warning, but from the looks of things, it would get worse. He glanced down at the man Jake had jumped. Thorne had wanted to talk to him, to find out what the hell was going on for sure, but the man had been unlucky. He shouldn't have turned when he did. His neck was broken. He was dead. Jake's weight, combined with the way he had hit, snapped the man's neck like a dry stick.

Standing up, Thorne started back to the house, Jake stepping lightly beside him. As he crossed out of the darkest shadows, the front door was flung open, and Brandy ran to his side, her soft brown eyes bright with the excitement just past. There was color high in her cheeks, and her breathing came in quick little gasps.

"We thought you were..." Brandy began then started over. "I mean, from the house when those cattle came through, it looked like..."

"There wouldn't be enough left of you to bury," Brandy's father finished for her as he came up. Angus slapped Thorne on the shoulder. "Glad to see you're all in one piece."

47

"That's a pretty bad cut," Brandy said, reaching up to touch the fresh wound along the side of Thorne's head. "You better let me put something on it."

Thorne winced at her touch. He had forgotten about that. "There's a fella laying yonder, he won't be giving you any more trouble," Thorne told Angus as Brandy led the way into the house.

Angus nodded and started toward the barn. "We'll just pack him up and send him on home so his friends can bury him proper."

CHAPTER FIVE

Outside the rambling log house it was cold. Night had passed and the golden glow of the morning was burning on the mountain slopes. The sky was clear and blue, unusual for a time of year when snow was expected in the form of a blizzard any day.

Harper Manning sat in a massive overstuffed chair before the crackling fire that filled the fireplace before him. His tall, wide-shouldered frame was immaculately clothed to include a vest with a gold watch chain draped from pocket to pocket, glittering in the firelight. Narrow, intent, with a thin straight nose, his face was like that of a hawk. His dark brown eyes were bright with a cold, hard light, and brimming with ambition.

He was only thirty-three, but Harper Manning had his goals set, and he was reaching for the top, no matter who or what he had to climb over to get there. Also, as others had already found out, he was not a man to go about things in a slow way. He meant to have power, and to get it, a man had to put

48

up appearances. Something to back up those appearances was also something he had to have. From his own experiences, Harper knew a man seeking power had to have land, money, and for the trimming on the cake, a pretty wife to look at him adoringly. For some reason, he had found people were not as taken with a single man as they were with one who was married.

That last part about a wife was where Harper got around to thinking about Brandy Mitchell. She was a pretty, fiery as all get out, but she was young, and he had no doubt he could tame her down into a real lady. Her father had flatly refused his advances, but there was always Brandy herself. Harper had had his share of experience with women, and imagined that if he worked it right, Brandy would go against even her father's will. They had gotten off on the wrong foot, and his foreman's raid on their place had not done him any good, but things could be patched up. Her father and brother didn't matter, it was Brandy he was interested in. Who knows, when he possession of their little ranch, he might even consider letting them live there just to keep her happy. With her on this arm, Harper knew he could hardly help catching the eyes of the right people who would be of use to him. And, he had to admit to himself, he was getting genuinely fond of her…in his own way.

Harper's foreman, Sonora Pike, the man Thorne had dubbed Snake Eye, was in the room with him, sitting in a chair with his feet propped on a table. Men like Pike were useful, but they added very little to the grace of a man's home. Pike had a pinched, sour-looking mouth, the upper lip fringed with a stringy black mustache. A swaggering, self-centered young man of slender build and small stature, he

49

walked with long strides, his body always hunched against the cold. His small black eyes were always squinting, and always moving quickly from side to side giving the impression of a snake ready to strike. Pike was a man who packed with him a mighty high opinion of himself, as well as his hip-slung six-gun and skill at using it. Though he appeared unconcerned as he sat near Harper Manning, that long and bony right hand was never far from his gun.

"Didn't see hide nor hair of that stranger I told you was with the Mitchell kid," Pike was saying with calm detachment. "I sure as hell would have liked taking him down a few pegs...a few of the other boys felt the same." Pike rolled himself a cigarette and stared over at his boss. He never had exactly liked Manning, but the pay was good. "Roy went on in ahead of the rest of us and slung a little lead, but I don't reckon he hit nothing."

Manning gave him a sharp look. "You don't know?" He bottled his anger inside and his words came out cold. "If the fool hurt that girl I'll break his neck." He made his comment as flat statement of fact, not a threat.

In an unconcerned gesture, Pike shrugged narrow shoulders and exhaled some smoke through his nose. "Now I ain't saying he did hit that girl and I ain't saying he didn't but whatever you're figuring on doing to Roy won't matter much to him. About an hour ago his horse come back with Roy tied across the saddle."

"I told you somebody would get himself shot if you went about it your way." Manning was angry. His voice was ringing with authority. He was playing the big landowner part to the hilt. "I didn't give you the authority for that raid," he snapped. "If you do something like that again without my say-so, I'll have to be looking for a new man to handle your position."

Raising a hand, Pike exhaled the smoke from his cigarette again. His black eyes were piercing, and one eyebrow was raised in irritation. "First off, he wasn't shot, he got his neck broke, somebody beat you to it, and that stranger was on the ranch when we hit. And, if you'll remember rightly, boss, the man you sent up in them hills to finish off the Mitchell boy ain't been seen since. Scott Mitchell come back though, and that stranger was with him." Pike paused, letting what he'd said sink in. "One of the boys up at the bunkhouse says that ranny goes by the name of Thorne Stevens. The way I see it"— Pike jabbed his glowing cigarette in Manning's direction—"he means nothing but trouble."

"What do you suggest?" Manning wasn't worried. He had grown too big for one man to be much more than an annoyance. After all, that was what he had hired Pike for.

"I'm thinking on it," Pike said slowly. "The trick is to find him first. I don't rightly know where he is, except that he's holed up in them hills somewheres." Pike flicked the remaining stub of his cigarette into the crackling fire before him and started to roll himself a second. "Seems like that fella, Stevens, don't talk to nobody, so when one of the boys gave me a handle to call him by, I started checking up." Pike lit up his second cigarette. "A while back I recollected an old buddy of mine sending me a wire a couple weeks back that he was a-heading in this direction with a small bunch of cattle and wondered if I could maybe give him a job here when he finished up with the cattle. He mentioned them cows was for a man who went by the name of Stevens."

Manning's dark brown eyes were fastened on his foreman. "I don't see the problem. This Stevens is one man, alone in blizzard country that kills men every year. You said yourself that no one really knows or cares that he's here except the Mitchells. He should be easier to handle than the rest of the ranchers around here. No one's going to miss a man they don't know exists." Manning made a broad gesture. "As for finding him, that friend of yours should be willing to tell you where the cattle are to be delivered. This ranch can always use another good hand."

Pike grinned around the cigarette between his lips. "I kinda figured that, Mr. Manning."

"And stop him before he gets started," Manning said quickly, "we don't want to have to go rooting him out later. It's enough trouble moving the ones who are already here without letting one more get started when we have our backs turned."

Standing up, Pike moved toward the door. Manning remained seated. Pike paused by the door, his left hand resting on the latch, his face stretched into a smile that looked pinched and cold. "Reckon I'll have to take care of that one with a rifle," he said over his shoulder. "That's one slick ranny. Don't reckon it'd be very smart of me to risk that Colt of his."

"It's your job," Manning said sharply. "You do it any way you see fit. I've got more important things to worry about than the details of your work."

Pike grunted and stepped through the door, letting in a swirling blast of cold air in his wake. The logs in the fireplace flared up and glowed brightly. Harper Manning glanced out the window, watching Pike's bunched form move across the ranch yard to the bunkhouse. Sonora Pike would be a danger to

52

him, Manning had no doubt of that. There was far too much that he had seen, and too much that he had done on Manning's direct orders for Manning to rest easy. Soon, when the opportunities he was expecting opened up, Pike would be in a position to blackmail him. What's more, he fully excepted it...if Pike remained alive. Pike was not the sort to remain a faithful lieutenant to Manning's generalship. He was a man who would be pulling some strings himself. It wouldn't be too much longer. There were only a few last holdouts. Then, Sonora Pike would be one loose end Manning would have to take care of himself.

As for the men who rode with Pike, most of them were wanted men. Those who were wouldn't risk capture to expose Manning, and those who were not wouldn't have the intelligence to pull something such as Pike could think up. Once Pike was dead, they would scatter, Manning was sure of that.

Manning sank back in his chair and dug out his pipe, filling it with tobacco. It was an unpleasant business, all this killing, but it was necessary. People died every day for a lot less than he was reaching for. It didn't make sense to Manning for a man to die in poverty, fighting for some unrecognized ideal, when he could live in wealth and position. Money itself wasn't important to Manning, respect and prestige were what he was after. He wished to become a mythical figure of a self-made man running a ranch the size of most states, and serving his state in the capacity of governor as well. Why, once he was governor, there was no end to the good he knew he could bring about. These few small-time ranchers he was displacing now was for the common good. There were always some who had to be sacrificed in a fight. And that's what Manning thought of this as…a fight for the good of all.

The smoke from the pipe filled the room with a warm, comfortable feeling, and Manning's thoughts turned to Brandy. His plans for the valley included her becoming his wife. As his wife she would be clothed in expensive gowns and her black hair would be piled high on her head in silken curls. It would be a far cry from the little hell cat that she was now. There would be no more riding all over the countryside alone, hell-for-leather in a man's clothes. She would be every inch the lady, she would have to be. Manning had decided her father was too lenient with her. What Brandy really needed was a firm hand, and Harper Manning was just the man to provide it.

Puffing contentedly on his pipe and gazing into the flames licking at the logs in the fireplace, Manning smiled to himself. Of course it took honey to catch a bee. Brandy rode alone a lot, even now with all the trouble. His men had spotted her several times, but under Manning's orders of hands off, had let her pass unchallenged. He didn't figure it would be too hard to locate her and talk to her without her father around to be giving an opinion. He knew he didn't have much time. The snow would fly any day. Manning regretted the move he had made with her father. Just by looking at Brandy he should have known that her father would be the type to be prideful and unbending. Left alone, Manning was sure he would be able to handle Brandy, and he was eager to see her father's face when he found out that she came to him herself.

CHAPTER SIX

Thorne held the reins of his big gray and stood ready to leave. Jake had already moved off a little ways. As usual he was itching to hit the trail. Thorne was feeling fiddle-footed himself, but he was intent on settling down, and Jake would have to learn to do the same. Still, the fact remained, Thorne was eager to hit the trail himself, and he wasn't unmindful of the thick, black clouds gathering on the northern horizon, hanging there almost stationary, looking as though they hadn't the power to move any faster. They would bring snow. How much or how little he couldn't tell, but in these parts, so late in the season, Thorne was expecting the worst.

Brandy was what was keeping him. Clothed in the pants, jacket, and shirt she wore when he had ridden in with Scott, Brandy was every bit as arresting in appearance as the first moment he had set eyes on her. The Mitchells had managed their problems before he had come along, and they would do the same after he left. There was plenty for him to do in the valley. It was Brandy he couldn't get out of his thoughts. The gentle softness of her hands while she bandaged the graze on his head. The warm, womanly smell of her presence mixed with the long-forgotten smell of fresh baking drifting out from the kitchen.

"Well," Thorne said quietly, "I best be getting on or that snow'll catch me on the trail." He settled his hat on his head covering the white bandage.

"I'll ride with you a ways," Brandy said impulsively, then she smiled a bit self-consciously at her father. "That is, if Pa doesn't mind."

Angus grinned. "Daughter, that there's the first

time you've asked my permission for anything in nigh onto eight years. Go along with you," he told her, "but leave yourself plenty of time to get back before the snows hit."

Flashing a quick smile in her father's direction, Brandy dashed for the barn. It took her only a couple of minutes to saddle up, then she reappeared leading a shaggy, roan-colored, mountain-bred pony who tugged on the bit and stepped gingerly beside her. Brandy swung easily into the leather, reining the paint pony around as Thorne came up beside her on his long-legged gray. Wearing his shaggy winter coat, the pony sure wasn't much to look at, but he would be tough, and all mustang. Those wild little ponies took to trails Thorne wouldn't trust to a mountain goat.

A cold bite was in the air as they put their horses to an easy lope, and left the ranch yard behind. As usual, Jake ran on ahead, and Thorne glanced sideways at Brandy. She sat the saddle straight and proud with the bearing of a princess. Cold wind brought the bloom of color to her gently weather-browned face. The wind pulled and caressed her shining black hair, whipping it behind her in a glistening curtain. She caught his eyes on her and smiled. Suddenly, to a man who only a short time before had felt time slip past like a rushing stream, it seemed as if spring would be an eternity away. He had hardly known her more than a day, but that was more than enough. Brandy was a woman who would stand beside a man, strong and proud. It was certain she was not a woman who would walk behind a man with head bowed.

For several miles they continued on together, talking about things that weren't important. The sky continued to darken as they rode. Finally, Thorne pulled up, gazing at the gathering clouds and trying to find the words to say what was in his mind. To explain the warm feeling deep inside that had started and continued to grow since he had met Brandy. Her pony was standing very close to his own gray, and Thorne could feel her closeness.

"You better start back," he said at last. His own steely blue-gray eyes held her bright brown ones. Thorne had never known any other way to do things besides going right to the core of it. "I'm coming back for you soon as the snow breaks in the spring," he told her quietly as a statement of fact.

Something flashed across her face, sharp and challenging, but then she softened again, and before she could open her mouth to say anything, Thorne leaned across his horse placing a kiss full on her lips. Just as quickly, he wheeled his horse and started for his valley.

"Reckon that'll hold me 'til spring," he called back over his shoulder.

A bit bewildered, Brandy stared after him, feeling strangely pleased with herself and a little off balance all at the same time. For a moment she was startled, angry that he would take so much for granted, and even a bit frightened. He was so tall, well over six feet. Weathered like some majestic tree, he was lean and hard, alone to face the elements year around. And how could she forget those cool, blue-gray eyes of his, telling her much more than words. There was a quiet readiness about him. She had no doubt that he had an explosive temper, and could be ruthless, even savage if a situation demanded it of him. But somehow, instinctively, Brandy knew he could never be that way with her. Something inside made her want to ride after him as she watched him disappear at a gallop up a draw. Reason somehow won out, and Brandy held her pony back, watching until there was nothing left for her to see. Wheeling the little mustang, Brandy started back home at a run.

Brandy hadn't left Thorne much more than a mile back when Harper Manning spotted her mounted on that shaggy little mustang of hers, letting him run. Putting his horse to the slope, Harper angled down the hill so he'd cross trails with her farther on. Finding her alone, away from her ranch, was a real piece of luck, and who was he to question good fortune.

Something distracted Brandy from the trail ahead, and she glanced off to either side, looking for what had caught the corner of her eye. A lone figure riding the ridge was making its way down toward her, and while she couldn't recognize who it was, she had better sense than to wait to find out. The little mustang of hers had been doing a lot of running though, and was about due for a rest. Shifting her course, Brandy headed more southeast, cutting a corner of Manning's spread, not knowing it was he who was behind her. Being edged off course by someone she couldn't even see was not to her liking, and what was more she knew only too well that the game little horse she rode was tiring. If the rider coming up on her flank had a fresh horse, there would be no outrunning him. As Brandy started looking for some cover she shortened her horse's stride. Only one good piece of cover came to her eyes, but she did have a rifle in the scabbard of her saddle, and she was not afraid to use it if necessary. She was not a very good shot, but at point-blank range, it would be hard for her to miss.

Harper saw Brandy turn in his direction. For an instant, it was almost as if they locked eyes over that long distance. Then Brandy changed course, veering off, cutting back toward what Harper realized was his own place. It puzzled him, but he changed course himself, still moving to head her off. His only intention, this time, was to talk to her, but it was beginning to look like he had a race on his hands.

Skirting the base of some hills that would put Brandy out of sight of the rider behind her, if only for a few seconds, she gave her pony his head and sent him scrambling part way up a gentle slope on the hill's far side. Positioning herself among some large rocks and the trunk of an old tree, Brandy stayed mounted and swung her rifle up out of the scabbard. She checked the load and waited. When that rider came around the bend, he couldn't help but run right into her. Knowing her horse would stand, Brandy looped the reins around her saddle horn and cocked the rifle. She could feel the cold bite of the air through the hot flush in her cheeks from the run. The soft stirring of the wind brought to her ears the rhythmic pounding of a horse's hoofs, a horse running easy. As the hoofbeats came closer, Brandy stood up in the stirrups and watched.

When Harper Manning came around that bend he couldn't have been much more than thirty yards from where Brandy sat her horse. If the earth had opened up in front of her she couldn't have been more surprised. Taking careful aim, Brandy put a shot well in front of his approaching horse. Despite the distance, the horse shied beneath his rider, side-stepping gingerly in a sort of shuffling dance step. As he pulled his horse up, its head shaking and snorting, Harper tipped his hat in Brandy's direction, looking no more disturbed than the prairie on a quiet day.

"I just want to talk, Brandy," he called up to her

59

cheerfully.

Brandy felt cornered in spite of the fact that it was she who held the gun. "Go ahead and talk," she yelled back, managing to keep both her voice and her gun steady.

Harper started to walk his horse forward.

"Hold it!" Brandy's voice whipped out at him. "You can talk fine from there."

He just kept on walking his horse slowly toward her. Inside, Brandy was panicky. Did he think she wouldn't be able to pull the trigger? She wasn't even sure of it herself, and his arrogant self-confidence made her even more nervous. When Harper kept on coming until he wasn't much more than ten feet away Brandy cocked the rifle. The little mustang beneath her stamped, feeling her nervousness.

"Well," she prodded when Harper pulled up.

"I just want to explain to you that I'm sorry about what happened at your place, and that I didn't know anything about it until late last night." He spoke earnestly, his face appearing genuinely pained. "I know this all sounds incredible," he went on, "but I didn't realize how bad things had gotten in the last few months." Brandy was wary, but Harper sensed he had her ear. "I knew there'd been some heckling in town, but I hadn't realized things had gotten so far out of hand. Some of my men, thinking, I suppose, that they had my approval, took it into their own hands to try and get me control of the valley." Harper shrugged as he threw an appraising glance in Brandy's direction, trying to read how she was reacting to his lies.

Puzzled and uncertain, Brandy looked at him. "That's a pretty big piece to swallow," she said quietly. "I doubt that there're many people around here who'll believe it. I don't think I do myself."

"You have to believe me," Harper pleaded, throwing himself into the part he had created for her benefit. "You'll see," he said, suddenly confident, a smile slipping across his handsome face, "there won't be any more trouble."

Frowning, Brandy let the muzzle of her rifle lower a bit, but still kept it handy. "You're serious." Brandy didn't know what to make of it. He could be lying, but she could not see what he would have to gain by it.

"I fired the men responsible," he went on smoothly. Remembering that most of his men would be spread away from the immediate ranchhouse for a couple of days, Harper told her coaxingly, "I'm down to a short crew. Why don't you ride over there with me right now and have a look for yourself?"

Suspicious, Brandy said shortly, "No." Trying to read something beneath the surface, she looked deep into his dark brown eyes.

The man she had so long thought of as a monster sat his horse before her, and he looked genuinely crestfallen.

Putting on a real good act for Brandy's benefit, Harper said with a sigh, "Well, I guess I can understand where you'd be frightened to come along with me after all that's happened." Smooth talk came free and easy to him, and he knew he at least had her doubting. She had spirit, and he was counting on that to spur her into coming with him. Given a little time, Harper was sure he could get Brandy to doubt even what she saw with her own eyes.

Giving him a sharp glance, Brandy shifted in her saddle. She couldn't help wondering, what if he was by some small chance telling her the truth? It was a small chance, but people got themselves killed in range wars, and that was a fact. Scott, Brandy was sure, would make it a point to be one of them. He was hotheaded and plowed into matters far too fast for caution. And, she had to admit, it irritated her to have Harper Manning think she was afraid. She glanced up at the darkening sky. The clouds were heavy with snow, and it wouldn't be waiting for her to finish her business before it cut loose. She could feel it on the wind, taste it in the air she breathed, and see it in the black clouds that hung like wreaths around the mountain peaks.

"I've changed my mind," she said quickly. "I'm going with you." Sliding her rifle back into her saddle boot, Brandy unwrapped the reins from the saddle horn and started her horse down the slope to where Manning waited.

The grin on Manning's face looked like it belonged to a foolish schoolboy with his first crush. Brandy had never seen the man like that before. She had met him only a couple of times, in town, before all the trouble started. Always, he had been the picture of cool control. His brown eyes had been on her a time or two when she had been going about her business, but it had never meant a thing to her. For an instant, Brandy felt a twinge of worry as her mustang made his way down the slope. She forced the thought from her mind and started for his ranch with Harper Manning.

CHAPTER SEVEN

It was still early when Brandy and Harper arrived at his ranch. It hadn't been a long ride; his holdings reached much farther to the east and west than to the north and south. All the way to the ranchhouse, Harper had been talking to Brandy trying to convince her that things had somehow gotten out of hand without his knowing it. Brandy wanted to believe him, it would have all been much easier that way, but she didn't. She was not quite devious enough to be able to read what he was up to, but the more he tried to convince her, the more suspicious she became. By the time they had reached the ranchhouse, she began wishing she hadn't come. It had been a childish mistake, proving she was not frightened of Harper Manning. Even so, Brandy reasoned, she was here now, maybe she could find out something that would help.

The temperature was falling like a rock in a clear pool when they rode in, and the wind was kicking up out of the north even more. The snow would be falling soon, and Brandy knew the treacherousness of Wyoming winters. There was still a long ride left ahead of her and she didn't plan to linger long. She slid from her horse's back, looping the reins over the hitching post while Harper gave an order to have the animals put in the barn out of the weather.

"I won't be staying long," Brandy said pointedly.

Harper nodded. "I understand," he said to her, "but it won't hurt to give your horse a little rest out of the wind, will it?" The smile he gave her was dazzling.

"Just make sure he stays saddled," she told him bluntly, and stepped through the door into the warmth of a large living room heated by fireplace and stoves.

Brandy sat down close to the fireplace while Harper went out and came back with coffee. He had taken off his boots and wore some kind of soft moccasins in their place. No sooner had he sat down

63

across from her than a knock sounded at the door. Manning answered it. A man Brandy wouldn't have trusted as far as she could throw him, came through the front door. Young with small, squinty eyes, a pinched mouth, and a stringy black mustache to frame it, he made Brandy's skin crawl.

"My foreman, Sonora Pike." Harper introduced him quickly, and the young man kept on moving across the room heading for a pair of double doors on the far side of the room. "We have some business to discuss that can't wait," Manning apologized. "It'll take only a few minutes."

Brandy nodded and watched Harper Manning follow his foreman into his study, leaving her alone, and wondering what business they had that couldn't keep in this weather. Quietly, she set down her cup on a table in front of her and rose to her feet, staring toward the closed study doors. Cautiously, she made her way in silence across the large room, stopping before the heavy doors. Beyond, she could hear the tones of muffled voices, but couldn't make out the words. Gently, she leaned an ear up against the wood, and immediately the words were clear to her.

They were talking about Thorne, about the small bunch of cattle he was having brought in, and about how they were going to stop it, and him. How they found out his name and where his ranch was to be didn't matter, they had done it. What did matter was the fact that Thorne didn't know they would be coming after him this soon. He would not be ready for them. Brandy took an involuntary step backward, her boot heel missing the rug on the floor, ringing on hard wood. Quick as a cat, Brandy darted back across the large room, pulling herself up short in front of the large window overlooking the ranch yard. All the muscles along her back tightened up and she felt cold as the double door to the study opened behind her and she heard the approach of footsteps. Not knowing what to expect, she just kept staring out the window before her.

When Harper laid one hand firmly on Brandy's shoulder she almost came off the floor in surprise. "You startled me," she said breathlessly, flashing him what she hoped to be a sincere smile. "I'd better be leaving," she added smoothly, staring at where Pike stood near the door. "The snow will be falling soon, and Pa will be worried about me."

Harper nodded toward his foreman. "You better get started," he said shortly. "She'll be staying here for a while." There was no need to pretend. He was sure she had heard everything that had been said behind the closed doors.

"I really can't," Brandy said a bit worried. "It's a long ride."

"I insist that you stay," Harper said coolly after Pike had left the house. "You don't think I'm fool enough to believe that you weren't listening at that door just a few seconds ago."

"Listening!" Brandy blurted out appearing genuinely appalled by his suggestion. "I wasn't doing anything of the kind!"

There was a calm, patient look about Harper Manning, a look that was masking a quick and violent temper. "It doesn't matter," he said above her protests, "you'll remain here overnight, and then the matter will already be taken care of."

Brandy's brown eyes flashed her anger and she straightened up before Harper Manning, her chin lifting, her manner becoming cold as ice. "Don't bet any silver money on that," she snapped, then spun on her heel, snatched her heavy jacket from the chair where she'd draped it, and started for the door.

Quick to follow, Manning put a restraining hand on her shoulder as her hand rested on the latch. When she depressed the latch and swung the door inward, Manning reached above her and slammed it shut before she could slip through. Then, from behind her, Brandy heard his soft, low chuckle. With only the pressure of his one hand on her shoulder, Manning turned her to face him. In that one hand, Brandy felt a strength she had never guessed he possessed, and his manner had changed from soothing to cruel and commanding.

"One of my men told me a few days ago that you were a mighty good-looking 'filly,' as he put it, but that no man had broken you yet." His voice was soft, almost caressing. "I'm the man to do it, Brandy, we're going to be together a long time. Who knows, if we get along real well, I might even let your father keep his land."

Brandy shrank back against the door but there was nowhere farther she could go, and he pinned her easily, almost smothering her with a kiss. At first she fought wildly, trying to break away, then slowly she relaxed as though in surrender. After a few seconds, Manning released his grip and stepped back, appraising her with a critical eye. No sooner had he fully released his grip on her than she turned on him like a wildcat, reared back and slapped him across the face with all the force she could muster, then darted around behind a chair before he could get ahold of her again.

"If you *ever* touch me again, I'll kill you, I swear it." Brandy was breathless, and still more angry than frightened.

A tiny droplet of blood showed at the corner of Harper's mouth where his lip had been cut against his tooth. The tip of his tongue touched gingerly at

66

the drop and a cold, distant light came into his dark brown eyes. All of a sudden, Brandy was more frightened than she had ever been in her life as she saw that light creep into the depths of his eyes. Her eyes shone bright and large against the paleness of her face. With even, deliberate steps, Manning started toward her, a half smile quirking his lips at the corners. It wasn't a nice smile.

Frantically, Brandy searched the room for some escape, but there was none. She had been a fool to believe anything Harper Manning said, but she had wanted the fighting to stop so much that she hadn't been thinking straight. Trying to keep pieces of furniture between them, she edged away from him, but he just kept coming.

Maneuvered into a position where she had only a single low table between herself and Manning, it happened. His hand shot out across the open space snagging her wrist before she could jump away. He dragged her around the table, and held her at arm's length, his eyes blazing, his handsome features twisted in anger. This wasn't the way he had planned it. If only she hadn't overheard his conversation with Pike. He had not been thinking. He should have realized that she would want to check up on him...to be sure. The damage was done, but even so Manning meant to have her, no matter what it took. It came down to a choice was the way he figured it, break her, or forget all his plans. He knew he couldn't let her go, he had wanted her from the first time he had seen her riding across the open range, her horse at a full run, her black hair shining and streaming out behind her on the wind. It hurt him to think of what he must do, but when it was over there would never again be any question about who was boss, and Brandy would

67

have no urge to spy on him again. After they were married, he would make it up to her. After all, he was a wealthy man, and as soon as she learned her place, she would be treated like a princess. What he was about to do was rightfully her father's job, but he had neglected it, and Harper regretted only that he had fallen to him.

Harper jerked Brandy closer, his eyes holding hers as she struggled in his grasp. He lifted his free hand, palm open, and struck her ringingly across the face. Her heavy bell of raven black hair swung around covering half of her face as Brandy stared in silent horror at Harper. Never in her life had she had a hand lifted against her. She twisted and tried to break free, but Harper held her fast with ease.

"I have to teach you a lesson," he told her softly, his voice deep and clear in the empty room.

Harper's eyes went to the vivid red print of his hand on her face. He didn't want to chance scarring her beautiful face so he doubled his fist and hit her in the stomach. The blow didn't have nearly the strength behind it that it could have, and Brandy knew it, but the pain of it jolted her entire body. Her breath was forced out of her lungs in one rush as her head came forward and she found herself staring down at the floor with Harper holding her up. As her eyes started to focus she saw the tan moccasins Harper was wearing.

In one wild, terrified moment, Brandy jerked away from Harper and slammed her booted foot down on the inside of his unprotected foot. Grunting, he released his hold on her, and all of a sudden Brandy found herself sailing backward off balance, tripping over a small table near the fireplace She fell heavily, the corner of the stone hearth catching her in the lower ribs. Brandy felt something crack and give inside as she hit the floor. Behind her, Harper was cursing and crossing the room toward her with hurried footsteps. Gasping in pain, Brandy lay where she had fallen, one hand touching the rough, splintery edge of a piece of firewood.

Realizing that he had hurt her more than he had intended, Harper said sharply, "Brandy!" a note of concern in his voice.

A grain of consciousness remained though Brandy's head was spinning. The roughness of the piece of firewood against her outflung hand was all she needed to know what she had to do. She laid still, praying that the curve of her fingers around the firewood would slip by unnoticed.

Heavy footsteps scuffed on the wooden floor as Harper covered the last few steps to where Brandy had fallen. She could hear the creak of the floorboards as they took his weight, and the rustle of clothing when he bent over her. The aroma of tobacco hung faintly about him as he slipped one arm about her shoulders, the other under her knees and moved to pick her up.

Holding her breath, Brandy had waited for that instant when Harper would be off balance and she would have the advantage. With fierce determination, her small hand gripped the end of the piece of wood, swinging it in a broad arc that ended alongside Harper Manning's head. Without uttering a sound, he slumped to the floor, unconscious.

Slowly, Brandy sat up, holding her injured side, and still feeling the pain from the blow she had taken in the stomach. For an instant her gaze rested on Harper, her eyes shining and alive with hate. She had sworn she would kill him if he touched her again, but now, with the cold-blooded opportunity lying beside her, she couldn't do it. Using the fireplace to brace herself, Brandy climbed unsteadily to her feet. Gasping in pain, she retrieved her leather, fleece-lined jacket from the floor where it had fallen during the struggle.

Brandy stood by the door, staring back at Harper's unconscious form as she shrugged into the heavy jacket, favoring her injured right side. Half sick with pain, she felt limp as an old washrag. To top it off, Brandy knew she should ride for home so her pa wouldn't start roaming Harper's range looking for her. The only trouble was, she knew what Harper was planning for Thorne, alone in his mountain valley. With that foreman of Harper's, Sonora Pike, and a few men, Thorne would be caught by surprise. He wouldn't have a chance, and Brandy knew it.

She had been up to that valley twice that she could remember. Once with her pa and her brother, and another time with just her brother Scott. Feeling as bad as she did, it would be a long, rough ride, but it was the only way she could warn Thorne. It was a journey she had to make.

Fastening the jacket, Brandy put on her hat and wrapped her thick scarf around her throat, turning the jacket collar up around it. It was going to take a lot of luck and nerve to get away from there without being questioned, and maybe stopped. Stepping to the door, Brandy gently lifted the latch and slipped outside, walking into the chill of the north wind. She made a conscious effort to stand up straight as she crossed to the barn, in spite of the pain that darted through her body with every step. Delicate snowflakes drifted and swirled on the wind before touching the earth. Brandy's only hope was that the snowfall would remain for some time as gentle as it had started. Walking as quickly as she could, Brandy made her way to the barn. Keeping the scarf pulled up around the lower part of her face, she went inside, moving quickly to her own little roan pony. She knew the slap Harper had planted on her face would be showing red, or maybe even turning into a dark bruise by now. If someone was in the barn, and he saw it, there would be questions. All that had occurred inside the house had taken only minutes, but her pony hadn't been worked that hard, and that should have been plenty of time for him to rest.

Hand on bridle, Brandy was heading for the door, when a tall, thin man appeared in front of her. He was older than some of the other men she had seen around the place His face was lined and streaks of white showed in his hair. Looking at her through calm blue eyes, he remembered that this girl's brother was the one who had been riding with Thorne Stevens when he and some of the boys had crossed trails with them a couple of days back. At that time he had tried to tell Pike who Thorne was, and his feet were still sore from that meeting. Thinking back, he shook his head, he had tried to warn that whelp. There were times when a man had to back off a mite and give things another good looking over before he went and did something stupid. But Sonora Pike considered himself a man to be reckoned with, and he had himself a lot of swaggering to do.

Stopping a couple of yards before she reached the stranger, Brandy eyed him nervously, not knowing exactly what to expect.

"Snow's falling," she said quietly when the man in front of her did nothing. "I have to be getting on home before it gets too bad to travel."

There wasn't much around the place that he knew

71

about except that he was working for fighting wages. Didn't seem like anybody saw fit to tell him anything. It didn't matter much to him really. He had him a pair of eyes and a brain, he figured most things out, given time. He was right canny, but he didn't need it where this girl was concerned. Something was wrong with her. He would have to be blind not to see it. She wanted to be moving on pronto, and the weather had nothing to do with it. He glanced toward the house. Something had happened up there. He half grinned as he looked at the girl. What the hell, he was drawing fighting wages, but that didn't include no women. Besides, he'd been told often enough to keep his nose out of Manning's personal business.

"Seems reasonable," he said quietly in reply to Brandy's earlier comment. Stepping aside, he swung open the big barn door.

Brandy led the mustang out of the barn, then stepped into the saddle, nearly falling into it. She caught her breath, then wheeled her pony, pointing his nose toward the mountains. With unbroken calm, the man watched from the barn as she left. He knew where the Mitchell spread lay, and it sure wasn't anywhere near where she was heading. Those cool blue eyes of his shifted once more toward the house. Something was wrong all right, but he figured that to be Mr. Manning's personal business, and he had no love for the man. He wasn't in any hurry to have himself a look, either. Glancing up at the sky, he noted that the weather was closing in fast. If that little girl was lucky, the snow would cover her tracks before anybody checked to see what happened. Silently, he swung the barn door closed, breaking off the wind. Manning would keep.

72

CHAPTER EIGHT

The sun had set over an hour earlier, and the snow was swirling on heavy gusts of wind. The little roan mustang of Brandy's moved along the rocky trail at a brisk walk, never missing a step. Cold and aching, Brandy sat hunched in the saddle. Though it was dark, and the wind tugged at her clothing, she never had a moment's doubt that the horse beneath her would get her over the narrow trail safely. Tough as old shoe leather, he was as surefooted as any mountain goat. Brandy and the little horse had been over a good many rough trails together in the past, and a few of them had been in the dark as well. Hoofs rang on stone as Brandy guided the roan close up against the rock wall and he rounded the bend, starting down the uneven downgrade to the valley floor.

It had still been light when Brandy had finally spotted the fan-shaped spill of earth that marked the beginning of the trail. A couple of times earlier she had thought she had heard the pounding of hoofs behind her, but they had never caught up. They weren't pushing as hard as she was, and Brandy was reasonably certain that they would not try to go in after Thorne until dawn. There weren't many who would risk that narrow trail bordered only by a rock wall and a sheer drop on a snowy, windy night.

First, the wind moaned softly, then it shrieked through the pass in the night as it gusted, then let up for a short spell. Brandy knew that below, the valley would be sprawling off to her right like a long, oval bowl cupped in among the towering mountains. Occasionally, in a lull in the wind, Brandy could hear the soft, distant bubbling of a stream. The ache in her ribs had gotten steadily worse as she had covered the long miles to the valley trail. She rode off balance, feeling the chill of the wind, and at the same time feeling the sweat inside her clothes. Brandy shuddered. Everyone who lived in those parts knew how easy it was to freeze to death, and sweating inside your clothes was one of the faster ways to manage it. Beneath her, Brandy could feel the pony starting the switchbacks that meant the end of the trail. An unexpected dip caused her to lurch in the saddle, and then they were down starting across the valley, shielded from the wind. She couldn't see much more than a few feet in front of her, so she let the pony have his head and kept moving. She hoped he would be true to his nature and head for the company of other horses.

A few delicate snowflakes drifted gently to the earth all around her as she rode, but for the moment, Brandy was grateful to be out of the pounding force of driving wind. The snow covered the ground here in a thin blanket, but it didn't compare with the howling wind-driven snow of the upper slopes.

All of a sudden, only a few yards away, Brandy heard Jake's unearthly howl. She half smiled. If the dog picked up her scent, it wouldn't be long before Thorne came to investigate. Pulling up her horse, she waited. Once again Jake howled, this time combining it with a half yelp of recognition. The big wolf-dog appeared from out of the darkness surrounding her. He sat at her horse's feet, gazing eagerly up at Brandy, then cut loose with another soulful howl that drifted out across the cold night air. Brandy stayed in the saddle, wishing that Thorne would hurry up. She felt like she was going to topple right out of the saddle. Leaning forward, she folded her arms, resting her weight on the saddle horn.

In what seemed like less than a few seconds, Brandy felt a gentle touch on her arm. When she half turned she found Thorne standing close beside her horse, his blue-gray eyes holding hers, looking concerned and puzzled. It was as if he was a part of the quiet darkness that surrounded them.

"Brandy," he said tentatively, "Brandy, what happened? You were supposed to be on your way back home." In the darkness of the snowy night, Thorne couldn't see very well, but it was plain there was something seriously wrong with Brandy. He kept his steadying hand where he had placed it on her arm, sensing that if he let go she would slip from the saddle.

Brandy felt drowsy. The cold didn't seem to her nearly as bitter as it had earlier, though the temperature had done nothing but drop. The pain in her side had made her forget the fact that she wasn't dressed warm enough for a night like this. It took her long seconds to organize her thoughts.

"Harper Manning knows where you are," she finally said in a slow, thick voice. "His men were right behind me most of the way up here." As an afterthought, she added: "I think I broke a rib."

The information Brandy brought didn't escape Thorne's attention, but for the moment his only concern was for her. The night was not so dark that he couldn't recognize in Brandy exhaustion as well as the first signs of freezing. Whatever else was wrong with her would have to wait until they reached camp. Slipping the reins from her hands, Thorne jumped easily up behind Brandy. He could feel her wince and try to draw away from him as he slipped one arm around her to hold her steady in

75

front of him on the steep grade to his camp. There wasn't any blood on her clothes that Thorne had seen or felt, and he wondered if her horse might have dumped her somewhere along the trail before she reached him. That was something that could always happen to any rider, good or otherwise. Thorne put his heels to Brandy's already tired horse, and the little roan took to the trail as if he were fresh from the barn. It was then that Thorne was mighty glad he had found a place so close to the valley's entrance to set up camp.

There hadn't been much time when Thorne had gotten back to his valley for any fancy work before the snow fell. Finding a sheltered spot and putting up windbreaks used up all the time there was. The place he had found was part way up one of the mountain slopes. It was like a giant cut in the earth. It ran for better than twelve yards, beginning at either end as no more than a narrow gash not more than a couple of inches high, and worked toward a small cave at the center. At the earth cave's largest point, it was no more than five feet high, an eight-foot gash back into the mountain, and only six feet of habitable space across. It had been perfect for Thorne's needs, and little time had been taken in lining the ground inside with pine boughs as well as erecting a windbreak angling across the northeast section of the opening. At the mouth of the cave he had built a fire backed up by a reflector of green logs to throw all the warmth into the cave. Snow had already begun falling when Thorne lashed the tops of several young pines together, and wove others into them to form a windbreak for the horses.

The fire was burning low when Thorne got back to his camp with Brandy. With ease, he carried her the last few strides to the cave, and put her down gently on his blankets that were already spread over the pine boughs. Without pausing for a second, he built the fire to a bright, crackling blaze and put the coffeepot close up beside it to warm.

Tired and aching, but still conscious, Brandy knew how important it was for her to get out of her heavy jacket and get the clothes close to her body dried. Awkwardly, favoring her injured side, she tried to shrug out of the leather jacket. Quickly, Thorne gave her a hand, doing his best not to hurt her. The icy dampness of her shirt made him frown in concern as he immediately bundled her in a dry blanket and insisting she remove her boots as well. Cold and wet, her feet were like a pair of half melted chunks of ice. Vigorously, Thorne rubbed them with a blanket warmed by the fire.

She wasn't in nearly as bad condition as she had first looked to Thorne out there in the darkness and snow. Exhausted mostly. In only a few minutes she was looking more alert and her eyes were brightening some. As soon as the coffee was hot, Thorne poured a cup and handed it to her, strong and black.

"What happened?" he demanded as he helped unwind the heavy scarf she still had wrapped around the lower part of her face so she could sip the coffee. Thorne cursed out loud when he saw what the scarf had been covering. The entire left side of her face was swollen and bruised. Brandy didn't get that from any fall from her horse, that was for sure "Who did that?" he asked before she had time to answer his first question.

Startled by the force in Thorne's voice, Brandy reached up and gingerly touched the bruised side of her face. With everything else she had on her mind during the last few hours, she had nearly forgotten the slap. The skin was tender to her touch, and raw from the wind.

"Manning." She answered his question shortly, sensing that he would recognize anything but the truth for what it was. Without wasting words, Brandy told Thorne what had happened after they had separated.

When she was finished, Thorne frowned. He was going to have himself a few words with Harper Manning soon as he got down out of the valley again, and the way things were shaping up, that looked to be mighty soon. But that would come later. Now he had his hands full just worrying about Brandy. Gently, he probed her injured side. That rib was busted all right, and with Manning's men coming down the pike after him, they would have to be doing a lot of fast traveling over rough country. Standing and fighting, was something he could not risk with Brandy to look out for. And, if anything happened to him, she would be either left alone up here, or Harper Manning would get her back. There was no law up there, nothing to stop him. Thorne glanced sideways at where Jake lay a couple of feet from the fire, curled in the corner where the windbreak butted with the earth. His head was raised, his green eyes intent on Thorne, and Brandy. Thorne smiled grimly. One thing was for certain, Jake was never left out when there was a fight, and if anything happened, it would be like trying to climb over the devil himself to reach Brandy. Digging through his supplies, Thorne came up with some bandages that would do to wrap her side tight. A couple of times in the past he had patched broken ribs. Each time it had been when a cowpoke got himself thrown from his horse on a trail drive.

Brandy didn't say much as Thorne wrapped the

bandage around her middle. The last time she'd had anything broken was when she was a kid and fell out of one of the big trees not far from their place. It had been a rib that time too. It had been worse than this, and there hadn't been a doctor for better than a hundred miles in any direction. Her pa had made do then, and Thorne was doing the same now. It would mend this time as well. Most Eastern folks would have been surprised at how much doctoring folks who lived in the wild, high country managed to pick up. Folks made do with what they had or they died. There was not a whole lot of choice in between.

Watching Thorne as he worked, Brandy could see the tiny lines around his eyes crinkled in concentration, and the deep lines of thought across his forehead. His touch was gentle, but there was little about him that was looking kindly. His face was hard and drawn in flat planes, his blue-gray eyes shining with anger. Thorne wasn't a man long on patience. He had a temper, and a quiet calm that had already made a lot of folks back up and sit down to think the matter over before taking him on. There was a quiet readiness about him, a kind of tough savageness, and yet when he looked at Brandy something in his eyes softened..

"You shouldn't have come up here," he quietly told her as he finished up. "You should have been riding for home."

Sitting in the earthen cave away from the cold wind and falling snow, Brandy was feeling much better than she had only a short while before. The stabbing pain in her ribs had subsided to a dull throb and, sitting before the fire, she was warm.

"I couldn't just let them come down on you without warning you," Brandy said earnestly. She paused and turned her eyes away from him, then turned back. "What are you going to do? Fight?"

Thorne met her level gaze and laughed bitterly. "Fight? For what? There's not a building standing, no fences, only a few scrub cattle. The horses can manage by themselves, my gray has done it before, and I don't reckon it'll be anything new to that mustang of yours. No..." He stared hard at her thoughtfully. "This time we're gonna run like hell."

"Run?" Brandy asked blankly, "Run where? There's only one way out of this valley."

Thorne grinned. "Over the top if need be," he said evenly, his mind made up.

"There's a trail?" Brandy's voice was puzzled, questioning.

"I make my own when there isn't one," Thorne said with a shrug. Picking up his rifle, Thorne started to go outside. "You best get some rest," he told her. "I have some checking to do." He turned to Jake. "Stay," he ordered the big dog before slipping off down the snowcovered slope.

Pulling the blanket even closer about her shoulders, Brandy stared after him. When he stood up, she realized for the first time that he wasn't wearing the worn black boots he'd had on when he came to the ranch. In their place was a pair of moccasins, the kind that lace up to the knee. He moved off quickly down the slight incline of the lower slope, being swallowed below by the darkness and gently falling snow Brandy thought about the mountains that surrounded the valley, and Thorne's assertion that they would go over the top. She didn't know if it had ever been done before, especially this time of the year, but there was no doubt in her mind that he could accomplish it.

Thorne wasn't near so positive of his ability as Brandy. Once before, many years back he had done

80

something like it, but at that time he had not had an injured girl on his hands. And he had sweated before it was over. Ironically, the fact that she was hurt was the reason he would have to try something as dangerous as he planned. Alone, Thorne would have taken to the slopes, dodging between the pines and leading them on a merry chase until they managed to kill themselves, or his own gun did the job for them. But he couldn't drag Brandy along through a running gunfight, and if he hid her somewhere, likely as not she would be found. If they got her, Thorne knew neither one of them had a chance.

Glancing up at the sky, Thorne half smiled. There were no stars visible, not even the moon could be glimpsed through the thick clouds. The snow was falling steadily. There was no telling how soon the pass into the valley would be blocked. To his way of thinking, the sooner the better. If the pass was blocked there would be no need to run. Skirting the foot of the mountain, Thorne moved off to scout the pass.

CHAPTER NINE

Just before dawn broke dull and gray on the eastern horizon, Sonora Pike started up that narrow trail to the valley. Aside from working for Harper Manning, Pike had a personal score to settle with the man who went by the name of Thorne Stevens. No man made Sonora Pike look the fool in front of his men. Pike had six good men with him on the trail and that was well over enough to handle the job, but this was one he wanted to be really sure about. There had been enough talk in the bunkhouse when they had run up against Stevens the first time.

Narrow shoulders hunched inside his coat against the cold, Pike rode stiff and straight in the saddle. He rode wary, his small, black eyes squinting into a pair of narrow slits as he peered into the early-morning gloom and started up the valley trail. More pinched than usual, his mouth looked grim, and his eyes held a piercing light. The men who rode with him were equally grim-faced and hard. They rode for Harper Manning because they could handle guns or cattle and they were more likely to be called on for the former than the latter. Manning had let it be known what it was he wanted, and Pike had personally hand-picked each man who rode the Manning range.

The horses picked their way carefully along the rocky trail, their shod hoofs occasionally slipping on snow covered rock The sun rising on a new day gradually lit the trail through the thick cloud cover as the seven killers cautiously made their way to the crest of the trail. As yet the pass wasn't clogged with snow, but it was plain to see it wouldn't take much more to do it. Pike glanced about uneasily. The snow had slowed to little more than an occasional flake drifting down on the wind, but winters in these parts were treacherous. It could stop snowing completely, only to start up again in an hour to reach a fury it had not possessed the first time. It made him worry a little, but not enough to pull back. Harper Manning wanted this matter taken care of before the man had himself a good chance to dig in, and that meant *now*. If they pulled back and waited until the weather cleared, it would be that much harder to root him out.

When Pike and his men reached the pass where the trail started down its final leg into the valley, the snow was better than knee high on the horses, and it was lucky the snow was the dry, light kind. Gazing at the carpet of whiteness surrounding him and his riders, Pike hesitated a few long seconds, then started down.

Other hoofprints had been seen by Pike on the trail before they had reached the rocky ledge that led into the valley, but here, in the newly fallen snow, they had disappeared. If he didn't know better, he would figure that the Mitchell girl was riding on ahead to warn Stevens. Those hoofprints were mighty suspicious. And their not being very deep meant that the pony wasn't carrying a heavy load. There was no one else Pike could figure for heading up to Thorne Stevens's valley. He knew, though, that Harper had the girl back up at the house. Pike didn't think he was fool enough to let her slip away from him. Besides, even if she had, how could she have gotten there well ahead of him and his men? It didn't make sense, but he was figuring on meeting up with more than just Stevens when he reached that man's camp. Perhaps Scott Mitchell had some cause to go riding up there. Whatever the reason, and whoever it was riding that pony, Pike wasn't figuring on them ever seeing the outside of that little valley again.

When they hit the switchbacks, Pike's horse slipped, floundering in the snow and ice. For a few frantic seconds he had his hands full keeping his horse on his feet. He pushed the thoughts about what lay ahead from his mind, and got to paying more attention to the treacherous trail under foot.

Thorne saw Sonora Pike and his bunch when they crested the trail at the pass, though he didn't know for sure who they were. From his lookout halfway up the side of one of the lower hills that rose on

83

either side of the valley, Thorne had first seen no more than a small, moving blob coming through the pass. The first blob had taken shape as horse and rider before the last had come through the pass. Thorne cursed. The sun was already well up in the sky, though the clouds, still thick, hid it from view. He had stood watch through the cold, snowy night, hoping luck would be running with him and the pass would be closed before the men Brandy had told him about had a chance to slip through. As it was, they were risking their necks, taking one helluva chance coming over that narrow, icy, trail, and that meant nothing but trouble for himself and Brandy.

There was nothing else for Thorne to do except start moving fast. Time was still with him, but not enough to be wasting any. He had to get back to the cave, collect Brandy and whatever supplies they could carry, and clear out. Thorne never was one to kid himself…their chances weren't good. The one thing he and Brandy had going for them was the fact that there just wasn't any give up in either one of them. How Manning's men figured to pull off what they had in mind was something he didn't have any way of knowing. He only knew what he was fixing to do, and that meant those gunmen coming down the trail would be walking into an empty valley. After finding that empty valley, Thorne reckoned they would clear out fast, or else they would be snowed in until the thaw.

Thorne had been away from the cave for several hours, and by now, he knew Brandy would be worrying about him. His footsteps moved faster, kicking up the loose snow in billowing clouds. It didn't matter how much of a trail he left behind for Manning's men. He would have too much of a lead for them to try coming up behind. Not many of their cut relished rough traveling on foot. Even if they showed no better sense than to try it, they wouldn't make it far.

As he approached the cave, Thorne slowed down, glancing around cautiously, out of habit. Jake would be right with Brandy where he left him, but if there was one lesson Thorne had learned well above all others, it was the lesson of caution. A man couldn't be too careful, it was often said, and that was one statement Thorne firmly believed in.

Jake's massive squared head was up and turned in his direction as Thorne ducked into the cave, the dog's green eyes intent on his master. A rifle muzzle was trained in his direction as well, but Brandy lowered it as soon as she got a good look at him by the fire. Thorne didn't remember leaving that rifle with her, so he knew she had to have gotten it off her saddle. He had left it just outside the mouth of the small cave only a few paces away. The wash of warm air over him felt good to Thorne when he got within the confines of the windbreak close to the fire.

Used to taking his rest where he could get it, Thorne settled down for a few seconds. "They're coming down the trail," he told Brandy shortly, the bitterness of all the past years of fighting plain in his voice. "We best get moving," he added. "There ain't a whole lot of time."

"Is there a chance they could catch us?" Brandy asked solemnly.

Thorne shrugged "Don't reckon so, not if we get moving, I doubt they'd be fool enough to even try."

Brandy gave a small, apprehensive laugh. "There's good reason for that."

Smiling, Thorne began putting together the supplies they'd be needing. "We'll make it all right," he said positively. "I've done it before." Thorne's voice was strong, assured, and he left out the details of that long-ago trip over snow-covered mountains.

Brandy was a strong girl, and Thorne saw it in her, but he didn't want to give her any more call to worry than she already had. There was no other choice open to them except to go over the top. He had counted seven men on that rocky trail into the valley, and with Brandy to worry about, he would not be left free to move. The mountain was dangerous, but not nearly so much as seven guns looking for targets.

With thoughts of Harper Manning flooding Thorne's brain, he made his way to the horses' shelter and turned them loose. They would make do, they had lived in wild country before. And this was the first heavy snow. There would still be grass worth pawing for. They weren't what was worrying at Thorne. It was the man who was forcing him to run, to leave his valley and fight again.

Harper Manning. That was a man Thorne figured to be paying a call on real soon. It would be no social call, either; it would be like the one Manning's men were paying on him now. Killing Harper Manning never entered Thorne's mind. That would be too easy. There was only one way to beat a man like him, and that was to break him. There had been nothing for Thorne to lose in his valley, not yet at least, but Manning had everything to lose. With plenty of time, the dark of night as his cover, and Jake by his side to warn him of trouble, Thorne figured to start taking Harper Manning apart piece by piece.

Thorne had come to this quiet little valley wanting only to be left alone. Instead, he had walked right into the middle of as much trouble as he'd ever seen before. They had brought this fight to him, and he was fixing to take it right back to them. It wasn't revenge he was after, it was an end, and there could be no end as long as Harper Manning held the power in these parts. Thorne needed little else to face that mountain with. He and Brandy would make it. There was no other way.

When Thorne got back to the cave, Brandy already had the supplies together. Most of what he had laid in for the winter would have to be left behind. They would need pack horses to haul all that out, and they had to travel light and fast. What they were taking was little enough, but it was all they could pack. Brandy had crammed a small flour sack with hard corn biscuits. A second sack, larger than the first, contained jerky, a little flour and salt, and some coffee in case there could be a fire later. Her jacket pockets were full of jerky and corn biscuits as well, and her jeans were heavy with rifle bullets. Thorne followed her example, filling his pockets. Then he hacked a hole in the center of the blanket she'd been wrapped in and hung it over her like a poncho, tying it together at the waist with a piece of rope. Few words passed between them as Brandy wrapped her scarf around her head and lower face, then shrugged into her jacket, buttoning it across the added bulk of the blanket.

The snow had stopped, and the temperature was dropping again. The valley lay white and silent at their feet. So quiet, it seemed like they could hear a twig snap a mile off. Under his fleece-lined jacket, Thorne slung a tightly capped water skin, counting on the warmth of his own body, trapped beneath the jacket, to keep it from freezing. It was mighty easy to get dehydrated traveling in cold weather, almost as easy as when traveling in the desert. Most folks thought it was an easy matter getting water in snow country, but that was a mistake. Eating crushed ice could cut a body's mouth and lips like a mouthful of glass. Just eating snow could make a man colder than he already was, or plain dehydrate him instead of slaking his thirst. A fire had to be built. Snow or ice had to be melted, or at least thawed enough to get the edge off. If a man was strong enough and the ice thin enough, he could kick a hole in the surface of a stream or lake, but there were times when there wasn't a stream or lake handy. It was best for a man to depend on himself instead of lady luck. Where Thorne was fixing to go, he didn't plan on making any detours to find water.

Uneeremoniously, Thorne dumped handfuls of snow on the fire, snuffing it to no more than a wisp of smoke. "Let's go," he said softly, his voice low in accordance with the stillness that surrounded them.

With no more words than that, Thorne hefted his rifle and started breaking trail, angling up the slope. Jake plowed through the snow with ease, and Brandy stuck close to Thorne, walking within the trail he broke. Silently, Thorne wished Brandy had never come, that he was alone to face those gunmen coming down the trail. If he were alone, they would never force him out. But, Thorne had to remind himself, if Brandy hadn't come, he would have had no advance warning. There would only have been Jake to warn him when they were already inside the mountain valley. Thorne shrugged. He had told Brandy he would be back after her in the spring, and he had meant it. There had been a change, but he did not want her any the less. It had been a long time since he had had something to fight for besides his own mean cussedness.

It didn't take much to get him thinking about that time back in EL Paso. He had fought for a reason then too. He'd had friends in EL Paso. Good folks with a little spread that straddled the Mexican border. It had started when Thorne had needed a job. Needing a job had been nearly a perpetual state with Thorne during those years. That was until he met up with Roberto Luz and his wife Margarita. In the beginning he had just hired on as a hand, but it didn't take long until Thorne was part of the family. It was a small spread. Most times it took only Thorne and Roberto to keep things moving. It was only during roundup that an extra man or two was hired on. Thorne had allowed himself to grow closer to Roberto and Margarita than he had to anyone else since his pa had died and he'd been separated from his brother. It was something he had sworn he would never let himself do again, but it had happened, and for a time it had seemed good, in spite of all his doubts.

Then it happened. Trouble came there just like it had every place else Thorne had ever lit. Seemed like folks never were quite sure of where the border was, and there were always plenty of people just itching to stir up trouble. Thorne had always been something of a hell-raiser himself, and was more than willing to give back just exactly what the other side was handing out. Roberto was a good, solid man who had always been no more than a small rancher, and wanted no trouble. There had been no way to explain to a man like that that there were others who were not so noble. By the time Roberto accepted the danger of his position, there was all-out war along that stretch of the border, and Margarita was dead.

Young, graceful, and raven haired, Margarita had

fallen victim to a band of murdering cutthroats that rode for one of the ranchers north of the border. There wasn't much left of Roberto after they returned home to find Margarita. The house had been no more than smoldering ashes, and Margarita lay in the yard near the corrals. It still sickened Thorne to remember how cruelly used and lifeless she lay like a broken doll, her once bright, teasing brown eyes dull and staring.

They had buried Margarita there, with little ceremony, among the bleak remains of their once happy home. Then Roberto Luz had ridden against the ranchers who had begun the border fight, and Thorne had ridden with him. Innocent folks had been killed and Thorne knew it, but it seemed like the innocent ones were always the ones in the way of the bullets. Margarita had been innocent as well, and it had not helped her either.

The border dispute turned into an all-out war, there was no law to stop it, and even less reason. Roberto and Thorne had ridden like vigilantes. For a time there was no right and no wrong, or even any up or down that Thorne could see. For a time he had been bitter, feeling little more than his own hatred. But, when the dust settled, and the fighting was past, Thorne changed. The heat of his anger simmered only inside, and with nothing left to hold him, he moved on.

Roberto did not change, and his name was well known across the West as a bandit, and one tough hombre for any man to handle. Thorne and Roberto had parted friends, but neither had known where the other drifted to. From time to time, Thorne still heard things about Roberto, just as he was sure Roberto heard things about him. When a man packed a reputation it was hard for him to travel

90

unnoticed. Something inside Roberto had snapped, Thorne had been sure of that the first day when they found Margarita. From different reports reaching him, Thorne figured he had gotten worse, and that there could only be one end for his old friend, a humble rancher turned gunslick. Somewhere there was a faster gun. He was only glad that he wouldn't have to be there to see it.

Thorne's blue-gray eyes shifted across the white slopes, picking a trail in his mind before them. The haunting thoughts of the past were swept from his mind like old cobwebs caught on a winter wind. He realized now the reason his insides turned at the thought of leaving Brandy alone. Margarita had been alone. Thorne faced the fear and pushed it from his mind. Once they were on the far side of the mountains, it would be safe to find a place for Brandy to hole up, and for him to do what he had to do.

CHAPTER TEN

The snow stopped falling about the time Sonora Pike and his men came off the rocky trail into Thorne's valley. Being a bit superstitious, but never letting on to other folks, Pike took the change in weather to be a good omen. And now he wouldn't have to ride with his head over his shoulder, always wondering if that narrow pass they had come through would still be open on the return trip. Going back through the pass wouldn't be an easy thing. Pike had ridden enough winter trails to know that well. There was always a chance that this valley had another, a hidden way out, in spite of its reputation, but if it came to that, Pike knew there would not be enough time to go poking around looking for it.

Pike's men strung out behind him, their horses plodding through the thin blanket of snow on the valley floor. Their shoulders hunched beneath their coats against the cold, six grim and surly men rode with Sonora Pike. They rode in the bitter cold, and risked the treacherous mountain snows for one reason…to do what they were paid to do. Kill a man named Thorne Stevens because Mr. Manning wanted him dead. Men of their cut rode the land like loaded guns, cocked and ready to go off just as soon as somebody pointed them.

A couple of them recognized Thorne's name, and they rode wary because of it. Stories they had heard said that Thorne Stevens was not a man to be taken lightly. A few years back stories had drifted up to Denver from down near the border about the man that would make your hair stand on end. Seemed like a two-man army had all but wiped out the big ranchers down that way, and one of the men had been called Thorne Stevens. Some time before that a man by the same name had been mixed up in some of the bloody battles that followed the early silver strikes in Nevada. Gun trouble had broken out even earlier in California than in Nevada, but the fight there had been over gold, and Thorne Stevens had been mixed up in that fracas as well.

The gunmen knew all that, but it didn't change what they had set out to do. The fight between the smaller ranchers and Harper Manning was the same as any other they had ever run across. Running across a man with a reputation like Thorne Stevens's was a mite peculiar in these parts, but the fact remained that he was no more than a man. A little more dangerous than most men, but still a man.

A man would be a fool, not watching his back when dealing with a man as easy on the trigger as the one they were tailing after, but that was no more than proper respect for one they figured to be one of their own kind.

Pike pulled his horse up and stared down at the snow around his horse's feet. There were a whole passel more tracks like the ones he had seen before they hit that rocky trail coming through the pass. Those prints were small and clear, made by a small horse, probably a mustang pony from the looks of them. He scratched his chin, not liking the looks of what he saw. If something had happened, if that girl was somewhere around, it meant nothing to him but trouble. To be sure, Pike would have to see the horse, but he had seen tracks like them before, and the only horse in these parts that would fit the tracks was that roan pony that the Mitchell girl rode. With one last glance at the tracks, Pike urged his horse forward.

It was the horses that Pike and his men came across first. They found the cluster of tracks leading out across the valley floor and figured Thorne to be on the move. When the three horses were found huddled together, their backs to the stirring of the wind, Pike cursed. That roan pony was with them all right. He should have known right off when he didn't see the tracks of that damn dog that Stevens kept with him, that they had lit out some other way.

Standing in the snow, holding his horse's reins, Pike gazed about the wide-open valley and the mountains that surrounded it. His small black eyes raked the distant slopes for some small sign of his quarry. Angry at being led off on a wild-goose chase, Pike did not realize right off that it left Thorne on foot, but when he did, his tight-lipped mouth creased up into a half smile. The pinpoint of light deep in those black, squinting eyes, and the tight smile framed by his stringy black mustache made him look like the devil himself as he climbed back into the saddle. His slight frame barely made the saddle creak as Pike wheeled his mount to face the men who rode with him. A couple of his men were left to set up a tight camp and to keep an eye on the horses, just in case Thorne and the girl had second thoughts about being on foot.

They were on foot now. Pike liked to think about that. It meant they couldn't have traveled very far in the snow and wind. And the snow that had been falling earlier had stopped. Their tracks would be plain. The only trouble with the whole thing was the fact that the Mitchell girl was there. Harper Manning wanted her, any fool could see that. When Pike had first drifted in he had sort of had an eye for her himself, but was quick to see which way the wind blew. If Harper wanted her, Pike figured he could have her as far as he was concerned. Money was a helluva lot more important to Pike than any woman could ever be. If they killed Thorne Stevens in front of her, though, Pike knew good and well they had better kill her too. Manning would never know what happened, nobody would. There wasn't much law in these parts, but if a man went to enough time and trouble, there was the Army some ways south. Out and out witnessed murder would be enough to bring them on up to investigate. That Brandy Mitchell was a little hell cat, and she wouldn't stop at anything once she got her mind set. For an instant the thought that Brandy had killed Manning getting away from him crossed Pike's mind, but he roughly pushed it aside.

It didn't take long to backtrack the three horses

through the snow to the earth cave where Thorne had set up a snug camp. A couple of his men ducked inside the tiny cave while Pike and the other two scouted around outside to see what they could pick up. It was easy enough to find the trail Thorne had left behind. Most certainly, he didn't do anything to hide it, and it led off straight up the side of the mountain. One of the men with Pike took out, following the trail a piece.

The rest of Pike's men emerged from the cave chewing energetically on the rock-hard corn biscuits like the ones Thorne and Brandy had packed along when they started up the mountain.

"That man's crazy as a coot," the younger, softer looking man who had followed the trail a ways commented when he got back. "How far does he think he'll get?"

One of the pair who had heard of Thorne Stevens in the past squinted at the trail blazed through the snow. Gnarled as an old tree and rough as cob, he peered at the younger man. "All the way, I reckon," he observed quietly, still chewing on the cold biscuits.

"The hell you say!" Pike snapped turning on the man. His hand rested on his gun butt as he eyed the man "And what would you say if I told you we were going right on up there after him?"

The older man gave Pike an all but toothless grin. "Why, I'd tell you to go right on ahead. I'll just mosey on back to the ranch, pick up my pay and ride on out. I hired on for gun trouble, not mountain climbing."

His thin lips drawn and tight, Pike grinned. "Ain't no need for that, Beckman," he said carefully. "I was figuring you and your pard could circle round, cut him off in case me and the rest of the boys don't catch him."

Sonora Pike was no man's fool. Those two wanted no part of climbing up that snow-covered mountain after a man who was liable to ambush them in the bargain, that was plain enough. Pike had a personal score to settle with Thorne Stevens, and he was going after him but he needed those men too much to risk losing them. Odds were Stevens would not make it over the top, despite what that fool thought. If he somehow did make it, Pike planned to have him cut off.

"We best get the others and get moving," Pike said casually. "Me and the boys will run him down before he reaches the other side."

Turning abruptly, Pike strode purposefully down the snow-covered slope toward the horses, kicking up great clouds of the dry fleecy snow before him. Before he had taken more than three steps the snow began falling again.

CHAPTER ELEVEN

High on the snow-covered slope overlooking his valley, Thorne Stevens squatted on his heels gazing at the country below. It was cold and still, with only the gentlest stirring of the wind. They were still well below the crest, and it was certain the wind would be strong higher up. The sky was gloomy and gray. The crisp air was threatening more snow. Thorne glanced around behind himself for an instant. In the shelter of some trees a little ways up the slope, Brandy was resting for a spell. She wasn't one to complain but Thorne knew that side of hers was painful, and her breath wasn't coming easy. It was plenty hard for a body to catch his breath on those high-up ridges, and it was going to get even worse when they reached the top, with the wind snatching it away. To make it worse, the air would be getting thinner as the climb got harder. With a broken rib, Brandy wasn't going to have an easy time of it. By the time they crested that mountain Thorne guessed it to be near twelve thousand feet.

For a time when Thorne had set himself down, he had been able to see dark blotches moving around against the white background below. He had been watchful for some sign that some of the men might be fool enough to try to follow him and Brandy. It did not come as any big surprise to him that some of them did. Five distant blobs were starting up in their general direction. Thorne didn't figure them to be coming far up that mountain slope, but then again, he didn't want to give them any encouragement either. Abruptly, Thorne stood up, striding quickly back to where he had left Brandy.

Staring at him as Thorne returned, Brandy's brown eyes were bright and large. "Trouble?" she asked quietly.

"Don't reckon so," Thorne said easily, seeing no sense in worrying her. The long ride, the hard climb and the cold was wearing on her, but he could still see the wildness and the strength he had seen in her that first day when he'd brought Scott home. There was still a fierce pride in the way she held herself, and not a hint of defeat.

The snow started falling again, and Thorne glanced once more toward the valley below. He knew this country, and if the gunmen didn't quit their fool notions and get themselves moving, they would surely be snowed in until spring. If that happened, it would be mighty interesting to see how many made it back out. A man had to know the country and bend with the storms if he figured to be living in wild back country, and from what Thorne knew of other gunmen in other places, he didn't think they could cut it. They would be at each other's throats like a pack of scavengers. Thorne shrugged unconsciously. They had forked their own broncs, now they could sit out the ride.

The big dog, Jake, stood up and shook the new snow from his coat. Thorne gave Brandy a hand to her feet and they continued the steep climb. What few trees there were this high up were gnarled and withered, bent in the direction of the wind.

Thorne was a thinking man, always planning on what might be coming next. Cold wind was gusting off the mountaintops as they approached the ridge and the cut in the rock just below it that would let them slip through to the other side. They still had some way to go, but Thorne was figuring the going down to being easier than the going up. As soon as they got back into the tree line below, they would be setting up camp. Brandy had to have a place to hole up, and he would be needing a horse. That meant taking whatever he could find running loose on Harper Manning's range. It wouldn't be too hard. Thorne knew the kind of sheltered places animals liked to use in bad weather.

Glancing northward into the dingy gray sky, Thorne spotted great banks of gray clouds, solid and dark, building up in the northern horizon. They meant more snow…heavy snow. The kind that could easily turn into a blizzard. He winced. If those clouds released their burden, the passes and cuts in the high ridges could be drifting ten to twenty feet deep in a day. When a storm cut loose swinging down out of the Big Horn Mountains and sweeping southward, the wind blew like a shriek out of hell. It swept high places clear down to bare rock, and piled swirling snow in heavy drifts wherever it could find a crack to hang onto.

Lunging ahead through snow nearly up to his belly, Jake reached the cut in the rock ahead of Thorne and Brandy. From below Thorne could see the higher peaks, cloaked in glistening white caps, stabbing into the gray sky. The ridge ran off in a darkening line in each direction from the cut Thorne was aiming for. Thorne saw the big dog stop in the cut, moving his head from side to side like an angry bear. They had been moving along steady, but when Thorne saw Jake pull up he knew without looking there could be only one reason, and that was that he couldn't go forward any farther.

Thorne ran the last few strides up to the rocky cut, dragging the thinner air into his lungs in gasps. Knowing something was very wrong, Brandy scrambled up behind him.

Below in the icy stillness a tree branch cracked as loud as a pistol shot. Thorne stood on the rocky ledge where the cut between the peaks dropped off into nothing but empty air. It was a good seventy-five or maybe even a hundred-foot drop from that ledge to where the mountain had a slope again. From where he stood to where the slope started it was a sheer drop. Dropoffs like that one weren't uncommon in those mountains, but Thorne had been counting on this not being one of them. A frown crossed Thorne's weathered face, and his hand went almost of its own will to the rope looped across his shoulder.

Brandy came up beside him and stood staring out into open space, the wind blowing her hair and tugging at her clothes. When she turned back to

Thorne, her eyes were large and round, her cheeks colored by the icy fingers of the wind.

Her expression was calm, her face serious. "What now?" Brandy asked him, her voice barely above a whisper. "Go back?"

They could go back, but that would mean a fight, and that was what Thorne had come this far to avoid. And Thorne had seen five men on that slope below. Where were the other two? He had counted seven when they came through the pass into the valley. His hand rested on the rope he carried. He could feel its roughness, and there was no doubt in his mind as to what he was going to do. There were a few rock outcroppings that would be heavy enough to take their weight. He took off his brown Stetson, brushed his shaggy brown hair back and resettled it on his head.

"No," he said finally, in answer to Brandy's question as he uncoiled the rope, "we keep going."

A little apprehensive, Brandy stared at him in silence. She looked up into his face, all browned and weathered. It was a good face, strong and angular, with high cheekbones and a determined set to the chin. His blue-gray eyes were distant as he worked, fashioning a sling on one end of the rope, and from time to time he glanced over his shoulder down the slope. Brandy had lived all her life in rough country, but she had never tried anything like this. She was scared, and she wasn't feeling too good, but she was determined not to let Thorne know. Trouble was coming up that slope behind them; Brandy could see it in Thorne's eyes every time he looked back.

As he worked, quickly tying the knots in the rope for the sling, Thorne could almost feel Brandy's worried eyes on him. He would send Brandy over the edge first, along with their supplies. Jake would be a different matter. The big dog weighed almost as much as a lot of men Thorne knew. Uppermost in Thorne's mind was the thinking about the time it would take. Pike and those men of his would be coming up after them. They would not have tried coming after them in the first place if they didn't plan on catching up, and that meant they would be pushing mighty hard. If they managed to catch up before they got over the edge, Thorne knew there would be hell to pay.

His words coming fast, he talked to Brandy as he worked with the rope. "When you reach the slope," Thorne said quickly, "there's going to be a lot of talus, loose rock that broke off from the cliff under that snow. If you try and stand up you're liable to sink in up to your knees, or slide halfway down the mountain before you can stop." He helped Brandy into the rope sling, and knotted supply bags into the rope with her. "So what you got to do," he continued quickly, "is lay down flat on top of the stuff. You'll slide some once you're out of that sling, but you'll stop if you don't go thrashing around. Stay right where you land 'til I can send Jake down and you get him untied. Then slide on down to where you can get some more solid footing and wait for me. You understand?"

Brandy nodded briefly and Thorne helped her to the edge of the cut. Anxiously, she asked: "But how will you get down?"

"I'll make out." Thorne's voice was unconcerned. "I don't plan on letting you go wandering around down there alone." Pulling on his tan leather gloves, he stepped back to one of the rock outcroppings and gave the heavy rope a turn around it, taking up the slack. "Use your hands and feet to keep you away from the cliff wall," he advised her, "and when you

101

get that sling untied, give the rope a couple of good pulls so's I know when you're clear."

Biting her lip in a way she had when she was nervous or upset, Brandy nodded in reply to Thorne's instructions and eased herself down over the edge into space. Icy wind stung her cheeks, and swung her roughly from side to side at the end of the rope. Even so, the feeling would have been exhilarating if it hadn't been for the circumstances. The wind was at its strongest at that point, stronger than anywhere else along their climb, but Brandy had very little trouble keeping herself away from the cliff's wall.

When Brandy's feet touched the ground, Thorne could feel the strain on the rope ease up. There was a pause, then a small shock ran up the rope to Thorne's hands as Brandy slipped on the loose footing. He gave the rope a double turn around the rock outcropping and held the end fast as Brandy got herself and their supplies free of the rope. Flexing the muscles in his arms, shoulders, and hands, Thorne glanced back over his shoulder down the slope keeping a wary eye out for varmints…the two-legged kind.

Feeling a couple of sharp tugs on the rope, Thorne hauled it back up, and adjusted the sling for Jake. Looking puzzled, the big dog stood quiet while Thorne worked, looping the ropes under his belly. Leaving a few feet of slack to start Jake over the edge, Thorne snubbed the rope tight around the rock. Moving to the edge with Jake trailing the rope that was tied to him, Thorne gave the big dog a reassuring pat and eased him out into space. Thorne braced his legs, and dug in his heels, though he slipped some in the snow, lowering Jake slowly down those first few feet until the rope was pulled taut. Backing off to where the rope was snubbed around the rock, Thorne loosened one turn and took the full strain of the animal's weight across his shoulders as he started lowering him to the slope below.

Thorne Stevens had done a lot of wood cutting over the years, putting a lot of beef on the shoulders of an already big man, but when he took the full strain of the big dog's weight, tossed and swayed by the wind, he knew he had a fight on his hands. He wrapped his gloved hands around the rope and lowered away, thankful he wasn't hauling him up instead of letting him down. Stopping for a short breather, Jake hung in the air like a trussed-up calf, and Thorne threw an extra coil of rope around the rock. Once again, he glanced down the trail behind him. Trouble was coming up that trail. Five dark blobs were silhouetted against the whiteness of the snow. How far were they? A quarter mile, maybe a little more. It was hard to tell with the snow still falling, and the distances distorted by the blanket of white. With renewed energy, Thorne again loosened the rope and continued lowering Jake to the slope below.

Brandy caught the top of the sling as Jake's feet touched the loose rock and snow Crouched flat on his belly, he just stared as Brandy untied the rope and gave it two sharp tugs to let Thorne know the dog was free. As Brandy and Jake slipped on down the loose surface of the slope, the rope lifted and quickly disappeared over the rock ledge above. Hanging onto their supplies, Brandy reached solid footing and stood up, watching for Thorne to start down.

Slipping one end of the rope through his belt along his side, Thorne dropped it to hang free against the cliff's edge. The other end he knotted fast to the rock outcropping he had had the rope coiled around when he had lowered Brandy and Jake. Barely finished with tying off the last knot, Thorne glanced up and found himself looking directly into the eyes of the man he knew to be Sonora Pike. Pike was still a good ways below the cut, but his gun came up as his eyes met Thorne's, and the shot cracked through the stillness, echoing through the distant mountains and canyons. Where that first bullet went Thorne never did know, but it didn't come close to him. The wind was too strong and the grade too steep for any accurate shooting from below, and Thorne wasn't going to try any shooting of his own.

At the crack of the first shot, Thorne dropped to his belly and inched his way toward the edge of the cut, trying to keep the rope from tangling as he moved. A second shot sounded on the slope but Thorne was hidden from even a lucky shot, and didn't pay it any mind. Them gunmen could waste all the lead they wanted. It would be that much less they would have if they crossed trails with him again.

Easing himself over the edge, Thorne swung free in the pummeling wind, one hand guiding his descent, the other breaking his speed. When Thorne was almost all the way down, Pike and his men appeared on the ledge above him. Bullets snapped through the air coming some closer than they had up above. Thorne dropped the last few feet, slipping and sliding in the talus and snow. Bullets were scarring the white blanket of snow like a sleet storm, and Thorne felt one tug at the shoulder of his jacket as he came up with Brandy.

The big dog, Jake, lunged on through the snow

ahead of them, making footprints in the snow big enough to belong to a small bear. It didn't take Thorne and Brandy much more than a half dozen strides to take them out of range. Knowing they were safe for the moment, Thorne pulled up and glanced up at the cut in the mountain peak. Standing on the edge, Thorne could see a figure outlined against the dark sky, and there was anger in its movements, but the wind snatched away the words. Turning away, Thorne started down the slope with Brandy. It would take time for them to come down that rope if they cared to try, but odds were they would not. If Pike and his men followed any farther, they were more than fools. The wind was getting stronger. A man coming down that rope now would be tossed around like a feather. They could never catch them now.

On the edge of the cut, Sonora Pike angrily holstered his gun, gazing at the two figures below moving toward the edge of the tree line. He cursed hoarsely as he glanced up at the sky. It was almost evening. The snow had stopped again and the sky was showing signs of clearing for a time. It was cold, probably below zero already, and Pike had been in this country long enough to know what could happen at night. It could probably reach as low as fifty below. Pike knew they couldn't follow any farther, not and get back to their horses before the snow cut off the valley but still he stood in the cut staring after them. His narrow, black eyes glinted beneath the brim of his hat, and he dragged the back of his sleeve across his mouth. Losing, or being made a fool of, wasn't something he took lightly. He was wishing hard that Thorne Stevens would make it down that mountain, cause he was planning on crossing trails with him again.

CHAPTER TWELVE

It was past dawn, the sun hanging low in the eastern sky, when Pike and his men dragged in off the trail. The fact that it had stopped snowing when he and his men were still up on that mountainside was the only thing that had saved them from being snowed into that valley until the spring thaw. As it was, the men were all pretty well done in and one had been thrown on the snowy, icy trail. He was busted up pretty bad. The other pair, the ones Pike had sent around to try and cut Thorne and the girl off, had run up against just too much mountain. There wasn't any way of telling which way Thorne headed after he got back into the tree line above. To top it off, there was not one really good tracker in their lot.

Giving up stuck in Pike's craw, but both the men and the animals were exhausted and nearly frozen to death. There were no two ways about it. They had to get back to the ranch for fresh mounts and supplies. Getting Thorne Stevens was becoming an obsession with Pike. He meant to get him if he had to follow him clear across the territory.

Pike had been giving considerable thought to something else as well as they climbed the frosty peaks wondering if that rocky ledge of a trail would be cut off, choked closed with snow. The men who rode with him might be satisfied to ride for no more than fighting wages, but he wasn't. The risks Pike was taking were getting too great, and the payoff to Manning too large for Pike to be satisfied with the crumbs from the big man's table. He had himself a real hankering for a piece of the pie, say about half. If Manning wasn't willing to go along, well, Pike figured he would just naturally have to take it all.

Piling down out of the saddle in front of the house, Pike had one of the men lead his stove-up horse to the barn. Sonora Pike was tired, but he had made up his mind, and he was feeling cocksure and tall as a mountain. Letting Manning know his thoughts wasn't part of his plan, but things were going to change around there. In spite of his exhaustion, Pike mounted the steps with his old swagger, and opened the door without knocking.

Standing near the fire, Harper Manning wheeled on Pike as mad as a she grizzly with young. "Don't you ever knock before barging on in?" He spat the words out as if scolding a disobedient child.

"Hell no," Pike retorted. "It's a waste of time, and damn hard on the knuckles!" His black eyes, no more than slits, slid around the room taking it all in. They stopped and held on that older man he'd hired on some time back, staring at his angular wolfish face. What was his name...Ben Colten. Pike remembered. He was the one recognized Stevens when they first ran across him with Scott Mitchell.

Moving a bit closer to the fire, Pike let his eyes slip back to Manning. "Let her get away from ya', didn't ya'," he sneered through a pinched, half grin. "Know where she is right now?" Taking off his gloves and stretching his hands toward the warmth of the fire, he went on before Manning could say anything. "Up on some mountain with that fella you sent us to roust out."

"What!" Manning exploded. "How do you know that?"

"Seen that roan pony of hers," Pike said casually, "caught a glimpse of her too." He chuckled softly, those coal black eyes of his lighting up.

Manning gave Pike a malignant stare. "You better be right, Pike," he snapped. "You damn well better be right." He wheeled on Ben Colten. "You said you were a tracker. Can you find him and that girl?"

Ben shrugged. "Sure enough can," he said quietly.

It had been hours since Ben Colten had come up from the barn and found Harper Manning stretched out on the floor near the fireplace, the fire nearly burned out. He remembered the girl. When he'd had the chance, he hadn't bothered to stop her, and if the same thing happened he would do the same again. Ben Colten didn't fight women. This here, though, this was something different. This was a job to track Thorne Stevens. If the girl was there when they caught up to him, there was nothing Ben could do about that.

Pike laughed shortly. "If all of us couldn't find hide nor hair of him, what makes you think you can?"

"Any jackass could track 'em now," Ben snorted. "There's two foot of snow out there, and he's dragging a girl along with him...hurt too, from what Mr. Manning here says."

His anger rising, Pike stared at Ben, his lips clamped into a thin, tight line. "You've been mighty close-mouthed about this here tracking ability of yours. How come you ain't said nothing about it before?"

"Ya' never asked me, boy," Ben told Pike sourly, his cool blue eyes staring at Pike from beneath dark brown eyebrows. "I best make myself real clear right now though," he added. "If'n I do the trackin', you boys can do the shooting."

Pike raised an eyebrow. "You scared, Ben?"

The lines in his face deepening, Ben grinned without humor. "Any time you want to, boy, you can try me." He glanced over at Manning. "I ain't fixin' to get mixed up in no shooting with a woman around," he stated flatly.

"Nothing's going to happen to that girl," Manning said pointedly glancing in Pike's direction.

"You say whatever you've a mind to," Ben said easily. "Just don't go figuring on seeing me around when the shooting starts. I told you plain, I ain't gonna have no hand in it." He ran a hand through his white-streaked brown hair. Rolling himself a cigarette, he lit it with a slender stick from the fire, and looked toward Pike. "I told you on the trail a few days back, I know Thorne Stevens. Don't reckon he recollects me yet, but he'll come around to it." He drew deeply on his cigarette. He rarely smoked, and when he did, it was usually just one for the pleasure of it. "Him and me met back in Nevada some years back. I was tracking for bounty then, and he'd just hired on to pull one of them mining towns together. We had words a time or two, but there were other things that needed tending more so each of us just walked wide around the other. But I'll tell ya', I seen him bring that whole mining camp to heel. He's a real curly wolf, that one." Ben grinned at Manning. "If it was me, I'd be mighty careful how I planned on taking his woman from him."

"Brandy's not his woman," Manning snapped. "And I don't want anyone forgetting who it is she does belong to."

Ignoring Manning's outburst, Pike turned toward Ben and breathed, "You *are* scared."

"Just cautious, boy," Ben emphasized the *boy*, digging at Pike. "And if you call me a coward again, me and you are gonna have at it." His voice was rock hard and cold as ice, but he never moved from his relaxed slump in the easy chair.

"How soon can you and the men ride?" Manning demanded.

Pike shrugged, his eyes still on Ben. "Hour maybe, maybe less. We'll be taking other men though. The boys I come back with are plumb tuckered, and Joe he's pretty busted up."

Harper Manning nodded shortly. "How about you?" he asked Ben.

"Suits me," Ben agreed. "I got nothing holding me here." He finished his cigarette and flipped the butt into the fireplace.

On the flats and the ridges the snow wasn't deep. It was in the hollows where it piled up near as high as a horse's belly. The sky was clear now, holding no more threat of snow, at least not for as long as it would take the clouds to pile up again. Manning was counting on that stretching into maybe a couple of days. When they came up with Brandy he didn't know exactly what he was going to do, her slugging him and running off the way she had. To Manning's way of thinking, that would all work itself out. She was his property, and he meant for her to know it. As for Thorne Stevens, there was only one way he could end up as far as Harper Manning was concerned. Dead.

Harper Manning rode out front with Sonora Pike and Ben Colten. Six others trailed along behind. They weren't more than an hour's ride from the Manning ranchhouse when Pike spotted two riders bearing down on them from out of the northeast. Pike didn't need a good look at the pair to figure out who they were. About now it couldn't be anybody else except Angus Mitchell and his kid.

"Look what's coming." Pulling his rifle from its

110

saddle scabbard, Pike nodded in the direction of the riders, and asked of Manning. "You want us to finish 'em now?"

"No. No shooting now." Manning said quickly. "It's going to have to look like an accident when they're taken care of."

Pike shrugged and kept his rifle in his hands as Mitchell and his boy drew their horses to a walk and came up to them. There was a change in Scott since that day Pike had seen him on the trail with Thorne Stevens. The softness had disappeared from his face, and the lines in his face were grim and set, his brown eyes hard and wary. A rifle was in his hands as he held his horse a little back and to one side of his father's. It was a sure bet that it was cocked and ready. He had seen the like before. Scott was past playing a fast man with a gun. He was backing his pa. If shooting got started, a man would be a fool not to figure on Scott slinging hot lead. Pike hadn't expected it in Scott, but he wasn't blind to it. Prudently, Pike kept his horse back enough to put Harper Manning between himself and Scott's rifle. No sense in taking a risk he didn't have to.

His black eyes hard and flat, Angus Mitchell glared at Manning. "I'm not a man to go beating around no bushes. Where's my girl?" Angus demanded. He sat his saddle quietly, and he held his blocky frame straight with a fierce pride although his eyes were rimmed with the red of lost sleep, the lines in his face deep and brooding.

Manning looked at Angus Mitchell with a genuinely surprised and puzzled look on his face "What makes you think I'd know where she is?"

Angus snapped impatiently: "'Cause she didn't come home yesterday like she shoulda, that's reason enough for me to figure you had a hand in it."

111

"I don't know where she is." Harper Manning remained unruffled, his hawklike face remained still, and his dark brown eyes rested evenly on Angus. "We're out hunting a bunch of cattle one of my boys said he saw snowbound on my west range."

"He's lying," Scott said savagely, his grip tightening on his rifle.

"We can't accuse without proof," Angus said over his shoulder to his son. Then he fastened his gaze on Manning. "I'll make you a promise, Manning. If I find something has happened to my girl, I'll find you and take you apart with my bare hands."

Flashing an easy smile in Angus's direction, Manning shrugged. "All I can tell you is my man saw her riding the northwest ridge with some stranger. I don't know where she is, but as for that promise you made...you're welcome to try any time you like."

Angus snorted his contempt, wheeled his horse and lit out, heading for the hills to the north with Scott right behind him.

"I still say he was lying," Scott angrily told his father when they pulled up within the cover of the hills.

Angus nodded. "It's a fact that smooth-talking, fancy-dressing dude wouldn't be riding out to tend his own cattle when he has plenty of hired hands to do it for him. Reckon we'll follow along behind 'em for a piece and see what turns up."

Scott slipped his rifle back in its saddle scabbard, and they cut back into the hills to keep out of sight.

CHAPTER THIRTEEN

The cold was bitter, but overhead the sky was clear blue. In spite of the weather's calm, Thorne had an itchy feeling it was going to snow again soon. He glanced around. Brandy was curled up in her blankets sleeping soundly to one side of the small fire, and Jake was lying quietly just outside the opening of the shelter. It hadn't taken any time at all to throw the hut together. How many times in the past had Thorne done the same for just himself and Jake? He had found a small grove of young saplings and cleared an area in the center, cutting many below ground level, and covering the stumps with loose earth. Then he had pulled the tops of the surrounding young trees together in the center, tying them fast with rawhide strings he carried at his belt. As many saplings as would reach from the outside edge of the cleared circle, he bent down to the center forming a tight domelike framework. Then, using the slender young trees he had cleared from the center, as well as plenty of pine boughs, he wove them into the framework, covering the hut completely, save for a hole in the top for their campfire smoke to escape. To complete the job, Thorne had packed the snow tightly around the base of the hut and thrown great armfuls up on the rounded sides. Another snowfall would make the hut seem like no more than another rise in the earth.

As he had worked, Thorne had glimpsed a pair of riders far below them. He had not seen clearly, but they couldn't be riding for anybody else but Harper Manning. Cross-legged, Thorne sat in front of the fire, gazing past the small flames at the white mountain slope beyond. Those two wouldn't be

113

finding him, he had chosen this place well. From below it would be invisible to all but the most experienced tracking eye.

Thorne threw a couple more sticks on the fire, then set to checking the loads of his guns. That last part, a tracker, was a thought that set him to worrying. More to the point, it was that older man, the one with the white streaks in his brown hair who had been riding with Pike that first day when Thorne brought Scott Mitchell back, who worried him. It seemed like he had recognized Thorne right off, but Thorne had not been able to place him yet although he had tried hard enough. Somewhere, before, he had crossed trails with him. Thorne kept worrying at the thought like a dog at a bone. There had been so many towns, so many mining camps, and Thorne had spent some time on both sides of the law. It would come to him, Thorne knew, if he had enough time to think on it. Was that man a tracker? If he was, Thorne didn't figure he had too much time to put a name to that face. In the past, he had known a few old mountain men turned bounty hunter. When they took to a trail, the only way a man could be free of them was to kill them. They were as canny as Indians, able to track a cougar across bare rock Thorne knew a few tricks of his own, but knowing what you were up against did more for a man than any tricks he might have picked up.

Brandy stirred on her blankets and opened her eyes. More than ten hours had passed since she fell asleep. It was good she was awake. Thorne glanced over at her as she stretched and sat up. They needed horses, and they weren't getting them as long as he remained with her. Thorne had managed to catch a few hours of sleep himself, trusting Jake to sound

114

the alarm if there was trouble about. Brandy had slept the deep sleep of exhaustion, and Thorne hadn't wanted to disturb her, or to leave the hut while she was still asleep. And Thorne had to admit to himself that while he wanted the horses he was somewhat reluctant to leave the mountain. The little snow-covered hut and the awesome size of the mountains made him feel safe. It made him feel like somehow Brandy would be protected. There were some Indian tribes that believed spirits lived in the high places. At times Thorne almost believed it. The mountains were always friendly to him, but he always figured when it came right down to it, a man had to fight his own fights.

Looking steadily at Brandy through quiet blue-gray eyes, Thorne handed her a couple of the hard corn biscuits that were still left. With a cold anger within him, he noted that the bruise Manning had left on her cheek had turned a dark purple. "I best go see about getting us some horses," he calmly told her.

Chewing slowly on one of the biscuits, Brandy didn't look too fond of the idea, but she nodded slowly. "Take Jake with you," she said quickly, anticipating Thorne. "I have a rifle and I'm pretty well hidden here. You'll be out in the open."

Thorne didn't bother to argue the point with her. Later there might be a reason, but for now she was right. Gathering his rope and rifle, Thorne settled his hat on his head, and moved to the little hut's entrance. "I'll be back as soon as I can," he promised over his shoulder as he left the hut.

As soon as Jake saw Thorne coming toward him, he stood up and shook himself vigorously. Brandy could see the pair of them moving off down the mountainside, their figures stark against the snow,

115

until the side of the hut cut off her view. For some time, Brandy pictured them as they had started out. The big dog, moving ahead of Thorne with a long, lumbering gait, his ears moving, and his nose constantly testing the air. Thorne had moved down the slope after the great dog with long easy strides belonging to a man who walked near as much as he rode.

A small patch of blue sky showed as Brandy stared out the entrance of the hut. She realized she had slept undisturbed by Thorne, when he should have been after the horses. The sun was well up. They had camped after sundown, eaten, and talked a while before she'd been able to drift off. More than enough time had passed to allow Harper Manning and his men to reach the mountain and to be already searching for them. Thorne was no fool, Brandy knew that, but every man who ever lived made mistakes, and he was no different. The fact Brandy couldn't get out of her mind was that he was only one man while Manning had what amounted to a small army at his command.

Absently, Brandy dropped a couple more sticks on the fire, then slid over to the hut's entrance. Snow spread out in a vast expanse, broken only by towering pines, and the footprints belonging to Thorne and his dog Jake. Bright and cold, the day held only a hint of dark clouds far on the northern horizon. It could mean more snow, or it could mean nothing. Brandy was starting to feel pretty good. Her side wasn't troubling her nearly as much as it had when Thorne had made camp the night before. She was still good and sore in more places than she realized she had. Even so, the long sleep had rested her, and Brandy felt as if she could take on the mountain again.

In silent wonderment, Brandy glanced back up at the mountain the pair of them and the big dog had come down. What they had done, she would never have believed possible. Going over the mountain had been enough to think about, but when they had reached that dropoff, she had thought they would be going back down. She had been terrified when Thorne had lowered her to that slope below, but they had it to do, and Thorne hadn't known her fear...or at least she didn't think it had shown.

Sometimes it seemed to Brandy as if she had been afraid all her life, what with one thing and another. There hadn't been anyone for her to talk to since her ma had died years back. When she needed someone to talk to, her pa always listened but he never really understood what she was trying to say. And Scott...well, just until a couple of years back, he was more to be tolerated than to be confided in. There had always been drifters, cattle rustlers, and the like passing through. She had always been a headstrong girl, so her pa had given her a fast horse and a rifle, though she had to be up mighty close before she could hit anything. Because of her fears, Brandy had bluffed her way through most every situation. Even Scott, her own brother, couldn't see beyond the front she put up. Her pa could though. He was always defensive of her, knowing more of what went on inside her than any other person alive, save maybe Thorne. She could still feel his blue-gray eyes resting on her, not seeing, anything, just kind of smiling, real quiet.

Maybe it was because of her fears that she was so strong. Being frightened never stopped her from reacting, from helping when she was needed, or from fighting when she had to. Brandy never gave up, and she never backed up. Some of that had probably rubbed off on her while her father had been trying to pound it home to Scott.

Brandy wondered about her pa and her brother. They would be looking for her by now, probably had been looking for some time. In only a few more hours she would be two days overdue returning to the ranch from a ride that should have taken no more than a few hours. They would be searching Manning's range. Brandy knew her father too well to think anything different. Scott, she knew, would be right there with him. She had done her share of worrying about Scott. Too much of the time he seemed more like a spoiled little boy, when it was well past the time for him to be a man.

Turning away from the emptiness of the mountain slope, Brandy moved closer to the fire. She sat crosslegged, her rifle resting across her knees. Except for the wind stirring through the trees, everything was quiet outside. All she could do was wait.

CHAPTER FOURTEEN

Thorne already had one horse roped and snubbed tight in a cluster of pines when he spotted the party of men strung out on the lower slopes. He couldn't make out how many there were; there were too many trees between him and them. Hunkered down low beside a broad pine trunk, he warned Jake to silence. Without a sound, the big dog crouched in the snow, his ears and nose testing the wind.

Watching for a time, Thorne could tell that the men below were hunting for sign. He watched them moving, spreading out, and coming up the slope.

The horse Thorne had tied in the trees behind him he had caught on the lower slopes. This time there would be sign for the trackers to find, and in this snow it would not be hard to follow. Thorne cursed softly to himself. It looked to him as if he and Brandy were going to have to manage with one horse.

Being a thinking man, Thorne wisely didn't take the one horse he had managed to corner and head back for Brandy at a dead run. Seemed to him that when they came across his trail it would be easy enough for them to follow without him helping them. A man thought clearly only when he took the time to think. Sitting on his heels in the snow, Thorne stayed where he was watching the men below. It was then he caught a flash of the older man who had been on the trail with Pike several days back.

And, in that same instant, Thorne remembered him. Ben Colten was the name the man went by when Thorne had known him, in days gone by, in Nevada. Thorne knew him now by reputation as well, as western men of that cut are known. It was his hair that had thrown Thorne. Quite a few years back he had seen Ben Colten, but only for a few days, and there had been no white in his dark-brown hair then. There were a few other subtle differences in the man now, all of them making him seem harder and more scheming than Thorne remembered. Ben Colten had been bounty hunting then, and he was doing the same now, with only a few small changes. He would be hard, if not downright impossible to throw. When he clamped down on something, or someone, he hung on like a wolverine. Thorne remembered that much only too well. To the casual onlooker, Colten seemed almost lazy, completely disinterested in what he was doing, but he always ran down his man, and he'd done it with cold, dogged, determination. Back then, there were folks who said Ben Colten was looking for death, that he would go after one man after another until he found his match. How true it was, Thorne didn't know. Maybe it was just another story tagged onto a man with a reputation. But he did remember those blue eyes so cold and empty. Ben Colten moved like a snake, kind of quiet and lazy in the sun, his eyes hooded. But when he struck, it was with the speed of a snake as well, and could be just as unexpected. A man the cut of Ben Colten was enough to make a man's skin crawl.

Thorne's sharp, blue-gray eyes remained fixed on the brown and white streaked head below. Far below, Ben turned slightly, and Thorne could see the distant blur of his face. For an instant, it was as if the man was staring right through all the trees that separated them, into Thorne's eyes. Shaking off the uneasy feeling, Thorne frowned. Ben Colten was a tracker all right, and a good one. A good tracker could almost sense when his quarry was near. Colten was nothing but trouble, the worst kind. Things would have been a lot easier if Thorne had his Sharps big .50 with him. With a little luck he could have worked his way to within maybe six hundred yards and finished Colten with one well-placed shot. Thorne wasn't the sort to shoot another man without warning, but this was one time he sure would have tried, and he had hit his mark a time or two before at that distance. But he'd left the big gun back in the cave in his valley, bringing only the lighter rifle, and the six-gun that rode at his hip. Even if he had the Sharps, it would take a lot of luck to get a shot through the thick stand of trees.

Standing up, the snow crunched softly under Thorne's feet. Glancing skyward, he noted the sun was straight up, and the blueness of the sky was beginning to fade to gray as more clouds moved in. The way things were going, he was beginning to wish those clouds would bring more snow. Already gone from Brandy for several hours, he was thinking of her being alone in that hut. Thorne was worried, he should be with Brandy. He did not want to leave her alone any longer than he had to, but he didn't want to lead that pack of coyotes back to her either, and he had left plenty of tracks already. Thorne had hoped it would take Manning a bit longer before he started tracking them, but that wasn't about to change what was fact now. For an instant he considered going after them, plunging in and letting fate decide the outcome. But, if he managed to get himself killed, what would happen to Brandy? Even if she found her way out through all this snow, and maybe a blizzard that might be coming in, she would likely end up back in Harper Manning's hands. With long strides, Thorne reached the side of the horse he had caught and had one hand on the rope when a blunt, sour-noted voice reached him from several strides away from behind another good-sized pine. Jake's hackles went up and his lips peeled back in a snarl at the unexpected voice. The man had to have been upwind of them for Jake to have missed catching his scent.

"Freeze right there," the voice ordered, and Thorne didn't need any time to place that voice. It belonged to the leader of that bunch he'd set on foot, the one who had followed him into his valley…Sonora Pike.

Not moving, Thorne stood where he was, and with a hand signal, ordered Jake to do the same.

Stiff-legged and bristling, the big dog stood by Thorne's side. Thorne would rather have turned Jake loose, but he didn't want him running into a bullet.

"That's showing good sense." Pike swaggered out from behind the trunk of a tree, giving Thorne a slow, satisfied smile. He was holding a six-gun in his hand. "Now drop the rifle you're holding, then the handgun, with two fingers." As Thorne eased his Winchester into the snow, Pike chuckled without humor. "That old man was right. He said you'd be going after horses, even said you'd be watching when the boys started tracking. That's why Manning took most of the boys and went on up the mountain." Pike chuckled again. "Me, I just knew where some of the stock wintered, and here you are." He jerked a finger toward the horse. "And horse stealing to boot," he said seriously. 'Why it wouldn't surprise me none if Mr. Manning takes it into his head to string you up." Keeping his hands wide apart and away from his body, Thorne half turned to face Pike, holding him in the steady gaze of his dark eyes. Pike was no different than Thorne remembered him. Like a baby rattler. His small black eyes were squinty with the hard look of ice about them. The stringy black mustache framed thin, compressed lips, and the air hung heavy with the feeling of death when he was near.

"You ain't dropped that six-gun yet," Pike prodded, gesturing toward Thorne's holster. "You best get shet of it 'fore I decide to finish you right here and now."

His eyes fixed on Pike's face, Thorne's face remained still. "You're gonna have to take it from me, Pike." His voice was quiet, his words clear as the mountain air.

Looking like he hadn't quite understood the

words that had been said, Pike screwed his face up even more than usual. "By damn, that's just what I'm doing, mister!" he exploded. "Now you drop that thing afore I get more mad than I already am."

There was a calm in Thorne's blue-gray eyes, and the glint of steel. Unmoving, his gaze remained fixed on Pike. He was counting on Pike's high opinion of himself to give him the edge he needed. It was a wild gamble, but it was all Thorne had. Sonora Pike was a prideful man out to prove something, and Thorne was counting on that something to keep him from pulling that trigger…for a short while anyhow.

Relaxing his arms a little, Thorne stared hard at Pike. "If you don't drop that gun you're holding and back off, you're a dead man," Thorne said easily. The whole time, Pike had the drop on him.

A raw, harsh laugh exploded from Pike's lips. "You're plumb out of your mind I'm the one holding the gun."

Thorne's expression never changed. His face remained hard, but calm and undisturbed. "Reckon you'd manage to hit me all right," Thorne admitted slowly, "but you'd be dead. If my slug didn't finish you, Jake here"—he nodded toward the big dog— "would tear your throat out before you could get off another shot."

Pike looked a bit uneasy, but he wasn't of a mind to do any backing down. In another few seconds, Thorne figured Pike would have worked himself up to pulling that trigger, but Scott Mitchell's voice carried firmly to the two men. Both heard him before they saw him.

"Drop the gun, Pike," Scott ordered in a harsh tone. "I'm packing a shotgun, and I don't figure I'll miss at this range."

The silence between them was so complete, Pike could hear the double click as the gun was cocked. Willing to take more than his share of chances, Pike was mighty cocky, but he wasn't a damned fool, and that was what a man would have to be to go up against a man with a double-barreled shotgun cocked and ready. Pike dropped his gun in the snow, his eyes remaining fixed on Thorne, waiting for the look of victory that he himself would have had if their positions had been reversed, but it never came. Save for the softening of some lines around his eyes, Thorne's expression remained the same.

Letting his arms down the rest of the way, Thorne glanced at Scott as he came into the small clearing. He was carrying a shotgun all right, he had not been bluffing. Some changes had taken place in Scott during the past couple of days. There was more assurance in his walk in spite of the slight limp he still showed from that slug Thorne had dug out of him. His face seemed harder, his chin outthrust with determination, his eyes flat and hard.

"You've got yourself a good sense of timing," Thorne said casually. "What made you come up here?"

Scott shrugged. "Pa and me trailed Harper Manning and his bunch up here. Pa figured that bunch they left down there was just to throw somebody off, so we followed the rest on up. When Pike here parted company with the rest, Pa and me split up. I followed him, and Pa tagged along after the rest of them. They must be near to the top of the mountain by now." With slow steps, Scott walked over to join Thorne, his gun never wavering from Pike. "It looked to Pa like they were figuring on working their way down from the top and maybe catching you and Brandy in the middle, providing

Brandy was still with you." Scott threw a questioning glance Thorne's way. "Is she?"

Out of the corner of his eye, Thorne could only see the side of Scott's face, but he could see worry there, and a brooding anger. "She's back up the mountain a ways," Thorne said quickly. "Waiting for me to get back with some horses."

"Horses?" Scott looked startled. "What happened to your own?"

"I'll tell you while we're riding," Thorne picked up his rifle out of the snow along with Pike's six-gun. The rifle he handed to Scott. "Here," he advised Scott quietly, "cover him with that while I tie him. You cut loose with that shotgun, you'll blow us both to hell."

Staying clear of Scott's line of fire, Thorne unbuckled Pike's belt, pulling it free and used it to lash his wrists together, his arms wrapped around a nearby tree. Pike glared at him as he worked quickly, pulling the belt leather tight around his wrists and tying it off.

"I'm going to get you," Pike stated flatly "I'm going to gun you down." He spat the words out like they were poison, and all the while he was turning a shade redder in the face.

Without comment, Thorne stuffed Pike's own neckerchief in his mouth and tied it tightly behind his head. By now, Colten and his bunch would be working their way up the mountain. It wouldn't take them long to find Pike and turn him loose. Thorne sighed. That little snake-eyed killer would be running loose again. It would be doing most everybody a service if somebody gunned him down and was done with it before he killed somebody else. It wasn't in him to kill a man in cold blood so he turned away and went back to Scott, taking

125

Pike's gun and stuffing it into his own belt as a spare.

Without looking back, Thorne stepped into Pike's saddle, taking the horse he'd caught up on the lead. Scott retrieved his horse from the trees, and Thorne took the lead up the mountain slope with Jake loping easily by his horse's side. Thoughts of Ben Colten kept slipping into his mind as they moved along. They were leaving plenty of sign for him to read on the mountainside, and with Harper Manning above, Thorne knew they would be playing cat and mouse mighty soon. Brandy, alone in that snow hut, was another thought that plagued him. It would have been better if he had taken her with him. The thought was pushed roughly from his mind. There wasn't time to doubt his own decisions.

"How many men does Manning have with him?" Thorne urgently asked of Scott.

"Nine, counting Manning and that foreman you just left tied to that tree, when we first come across 'em on the trail. They picked up some more along the trail somewheres while Pa and me were cutting through the hills though, 'cause the last time we got us a clear look there was maybe eighteen." Scott gave Thorne a slow grin. "Looks like somebody thinks real high of your ability with that gun you pack."

Thorne let Scott's statement slide past without comment. That would be Ben Colten wanting so many men. He would split them up in groups and cover the area faster. But he would somehow manage to be there when they ran the quarry down, providing they did. That was Colten's style. Thorne knew they'd have to stop running sometime, but he wanted to be able to pick the place and the time. A man stayed alive by staying out of corners he

126

couldn't get himself out of.

The air was so fresh a man could almost taste it, and the chill that rode on the softly blowing winds was unmistakable. There would be more snow soon. Dark, heavy clouds were boiling across the sky. The younger pines on the slopes seemed to shiver even before the north wind struck. Thorne sent his horse along a little faster, with Scott coming along behind, picking up stride with him. The distance he'd gone seemed so much farther coming back than it had when he had left. Thorne's face was set and hard.

CHAPTER FIFTEEN

Flames at the wood piled on the small campfire as Brandy sat in the snow hut, quietly watching. The firelight shimmered through her thick black hair and shone in the depths of her bright brown eyes. It was warm in the little hut, but outside the sky was growing darker by the minute. The wind was picking up a little, like it was testing its strength on the pines, moaning softly through their branches. Wolves could be heard howling to each other some distance off. They would be trying to get back together before the snow fell again. From observation, Brandy had learned that wolves had a strong pack instinct. If the feel of snow was in the air they would forget about hunting, and try to get back with their mates and pups before the snow cut them off. Brandy had seen it before, two or three full-grown wolves passing up a snowbound cow, an easy kill, heading in the direction of a distant howl of another wolf. It seemed like the snow didn't usually take long after that to start falling.

Earlier, Brandy had seen some elk pass through the clearing beyond the little hut, but they were gone now. Only the sound of the wind in the trees, and the skittering sound of small paws running for shelter reached her ears.

Then, there was something else, something that seemed out of place. Brandy listened closer, her rifle gripped tightly in her hands. It couldn't be Thorne. Why she knew the sounds she heard belonged to people Brandy wasn't exactly sure, but she did know. Straining to hear whatever it was that had drawn her attention, she moved to the hut's opening and remained perfectly still. Her every movement betrayed her nervousness.

Brandy listened intently and then the sound came again. It was a voice, the words weren't plain, and then there was more than one. Feeling a moment of panic, Brandy cringed and pulled back inside the hut. Steeling herself, she forced herself to think. Whoever was out there would find the hut; there hadn't been enough snow to hide it completely. It had to be some of Harper Manning's men. They were the only ones who would be moving around on the mountain, giving little thought to the noise they made in passing. Thorne moved through the trees like an Indian and with danger so near, he would speak in no more than a murmur.

Voices reached her ears again, this time closer and with them was the sound of a hooffall on stone as well. Brandy snatched up the sacks of food and her rifle. She couldn't stay where she was, they were coming too close. Pausing only for a moment to glance quickly around outside, Brandy slipped out of the hut, heading into the trees.

Angling down the slope, choosing the same trail Thorne had used before her, Brandy ran a piece, putting some distance between herself and the approaching riders. It wouldn't take an Indian tracker to follow her in this snow, but she kept panic from her thoughts and moved steadily on. Her breath was coming short and fast from the injury to her side, forcing Brandy to slow to a fast walk. Towering pines were everywhere on the mountain slope as well as an occasional aspen grove. Deliberately, she moved in front of the larger trees, trying to keep them between herself and the hut Thorne had erected. If her movements caught their eyes, they would not have to go to the trouble of following a trail. She kept a close eye out for Thorne's trail in the snow, and kept her own running parallel to it. Faint sounds of voices behind her carried on the clear mountain air. Gasping, Brandy held up for a few seconds in a clump of aspen to catch her breath. In the past, she'd covered a lot of miles on foot, once better than twelve miles in riding boots when her horse threw her, but never with a broken rib and feeling like half the territory was after her. The aspens were good shelter, and she had her rifle in hand. For a short time, she would rest and watch, then cut back through the aspens and double back to pick up Thorne's trail.

Later, when Thorne and Scott reached the little clearing and the snow hut, Thorne didn't need anyone to tell him Brandy wasn't there. There was an empty feeling to the place, even as they circled it at the clearing's southern edge. Jake was snarling, his hackles raised, his nose testing the air. Scott pulled his horse up alongside Thorne's. He was packing his shotgun again, both barrels loaded and ready.

"Something wrong?" Scott asked frowning.

Thorne nodded, his face grim. "She's not here."

He glanced down at Jake who was growling low in his throat and standing stiff-legged close beside Thorne's mount. "He figures there's something wrong too." He indicated the big dog and stepped down from his mount, handing Scott the reins. "Reckon I'd better see what happened."

Scott started to say something, but Thorne was already down, and walking warily toward the snow hut, Jake close beside him. Expecting trouble here as he had so many times before in all those other towns and ranches, Thorne had his gun out and ready. But this time there was a difference. There was Brandy.

Cautiously, Thorne moved forward, casting his glance about the snow-covered ground. There were tracks, a lot of them, but it didn't look to him like there'd been any struggle, and Brandy, he well knew, would fight. Her small bootprints were mixed up with the others. Brandy had to have smelled trouble, and moved out before the riders that made the other tracks had come in. There was an unsettling feeling about the place. Thorne could feel it, and Jake was telling him there was someone nearby. The big dog was right, of that Thorne had no doubt, but he had to know what happened if he was to find Brandy. That she had left alone, Thorne was sure, but how long before he had come back?

Thorne ducked into the hut, and examined the remains of the campfire. The coals weren't even cool yet. Sitting back on his heels, Thorne took a moment to think. He had known Brandy only a short time, but he knew pretty well how she thought. She'd be following the trail he had left when he went after the horses, figuring to either catch up or meet him coming back. Because of that rib, she would tire easily, and moving thorough the snow

130

would be slow work. Even so, Thorne figured they had better move fast if they wanted to catch up with her before Brandy managed to run right into the bunch Harper Manning had left below. Stooped over, Thorne went back outside.

The first shot slapped into the snow a couple of inches from his boot toe. Thorne dropped into the snow, rolling for the cover of a tree trunk, then all hell broke loose. Bullets kicked up the snow beside Thorne as he rolled, like a swarm of angry hornets. His six-gun leaped into his hand, spitting lead in return, as he reached cover. A bullet slapped into the tree trunk throwing splinters into his face, and off to one side he saw Scott go off his horse, and land hard. He was hit, but scrambling for cover, still holding onto that shotgun as Thorne managed to lay down some cover for him. The horses moved off a few yards out of the line of fire. When Thorne glanced after Scott he could see bright crimson blotches in the snow where he had passed. Thorne's face was set and grim. He hoped Scott had enough good sense to get that hole plugged on his own.

The thought had no more than crossed Thorne's mind than Scott's shotgun roared and a strangled scream reached his ears from the stand of young pines on the far side of the little clearing. And Scott, Thorne knew, had used only one barrel. The other would still be packing its load, and Scott would as likely as not have a few more shells in his pockets as well as the six-gun at his hip. He wouldn't have to be a good shot with a shotgun, just point the dad-blamed thing and pull the trigger. There was no more to it than that, but it packed an awful wallop, and it had taught many men proper respect for it.

For a moment silence settled over the clearing, though the smell of gunpowder still hung on the crisp, cold air. Thorne thought he heard a moan from somewheres, but he couldn't rightly place it. Besides, he wasn't interested in putting another hole in an already wounded man. To Thorne's way of thinking, the key to this situation was Harper Manning. Get a slug in that one, and the rest would drift. There wouldn't be anything to hold them. Thorne figured he would recognize Manning if he saw him, Brandy had told him as much. Manning was known to be a tall, sharp-dressing dandy with the hard, lined face of a hawk. He shouldn't be hard to spot if he showed himself.

All of a sudden Thorne decided it had been quiet too long. The bushwhackers in the trees would be figuring a way to work their way around and come up on both himself and Scott from behind. He threw a few quick shots into the trees to sort of let their minds go on figuring him to be in the same place, then edged his way up the slope, reloading as he went. Jake slunk along beside him, continuing on a little farther when Thorne pulled up again to wait. The dog was onto something; Thorne could hear him moving off. He was circling, moving off with all the craft and cunning of the wolf that was in him.

Thorne cursed softly to himself. He had left his rifle on his horse. All he had was the six-gun that hung from his hip and a knife in its sheath at his belt. There was no way to be sure how many men were out there, but from what Scott had been telling him coming up the trail, Thorne figured there had to be at least ten or twelve. He had been in enough fights to know his position wasn't good. His field of vision was limited, his enemy knew about where he was, and Scott was wounded, there was no telling how bad. To top it off, he didn't know where Brandy was.

Edging back under the cover of the ground sweeping limbs of an old pine, Thorne let his gaze move over the stand of trees opposite him. There was a flash of movement and color, Thorne snapped off a couple of shots, not able to tell for sure if he'd hit anything. Then, something moved close behind him. Instinctively, he turned, bringing his gun up and squeezing off a shot all in the same blurred movement. There were two of them, something Thorne could not see in that instant when he felt movement behind him. His slug took the closer one high in the chest, spinning him around and throwing him face down into a high snowdrift backed up against one of the low pine limbs. A sharp, burning pain shot along Thorne's left shoulder close to his neck as the second man's gun exploded. Only Thorne's quick movement to fire had saved him, and now he was off balance, looking down the black cave of the second man's gun barrel.

From only a few feet to the gunman's left there came a low, deep-throated growl, and then Jake came out of the tangle of tree limbs like a wounded grizzly. Lips peeled back in a deadly snarl, the huge dog lunged, bowling the man over in the snow. The gun in the man's hand exploded, the slug going wide past Thorne's head, and all of a sudden the paid killer found himself fighting for his own life beneath better than one hundred-fifty pounds of killing mad wolf-dog.

Green eyes glowing, and teeth snapping, Jake was all over the man as they rolled together in the snow, the gunman for a moment successfully blocking shining white teeth from his throat. Thorne rolled to his knees and laid his gun barrel across the man's head, ending the fight. Panting, Jake stepped back, his eyes ablaze with hate. Thorne glanced down at the man in the snow. Jake had managed to cut him up pretty bad, but it didn't appear to be fatal. As Thorne collected the guns from the fallen men he found the one he had shot was dead.

With Jake close beside him, Thorne moved back down the slope, working his way in Scott's direction. For the first time since the shooting, Thorne was aware of the warm, sticky wetness inside his coat that was his own blood. He held up for a moment, checking the wound. It was a graze, a deep furrow had been cut by the bullet across the top of his shoulder from front to back. Quickly finding some moss, Thorne tied it in place with his neckerchief to stop the bleeding, then moved on. His wound was not much more than a scratch, but he had seen the way Scott came off his horse, and he didn't figure him to be that lucky.

The trees were pretty thick along the route Thorne had chosen, but even so he drew a couple of slugs as he covered the ground between him and Scott. Trying to figure a way across the open ground that didn't include getting himself shot, Thorne drew up on the edge of the clearing. For a moment he sat on his heels, thinking. He had not heard the roar of the shotgun for several minutes. A couple of hired guns were spotted by Thorne moving through the trees only a short distance from him, but he held his fire. He wasn't about to give away his position before he was ready to make a move. His blue-gray eyes were alert, and every muscle in his body was taut as wet rawhide.

Thorne was on his feet, bent over to make a run for Scott when a rifle spoke from higher up the slope. Shots cracked loudly in the mountain air, coming close together and fast as pistol shots. Whoever was shooting was up high, probably in the rocks, and was able to spot his targets. It took only a few shots for Thorne to realize that he and Scott weren't the targets. The guns on the far side of the little clearing spat flame in answer to the long gun's rapid tattoo. Thorne started for Scott with a lunge. Off to one side he heard a man scream, and another shout hoarse orders. The only place where a man could have the field of fire that man had was from behind some rocks a little ways up the trail. Thorne figured that it had to be Angus Mitchell, Scott's pa.

Crossing to where Scott was holed up with about five good strides, Thorne pulled up knee-deep in snow, just short of Scott's shotgun. Jake growled low in his throat at the sight of the shotgun, but Thorne quieted him with a word and dropped to one knee in the snow beside Scott.

Scott threw him a quick, pained grin. "Wondered how long it'd take you to get yourself back here." Pain was in his dark-brown eyes, and the wariness of a hunted man, but the scared kid Thorne had first met no longer lurked behind the rest.

Thorne eased Scott over onto his back from where he had been sprawled on his belly behind the partial shelter of a deadfall. He'd made a mighty fine target sitting up there on his horse near out in the open, and that first slug had caught him hard on the right side below his ribcage. Where he had lain, the snow was covered a bright red with his blood. Easing back his coat and shirt, Thorne flinched at the sight of the wound. As near as he could recall, he had seen only two others as bad without the man already being dead. One had lived, the other hadn't. It looked to Thorne like Scott was going to get a chance to break the tie. Quickly, holstering his gun, Thorne dug deep in the snow beside a tree reaching for the moss that grew there. He moved back to

135

Scott, the sound of gunfire still loud in his ears, and used the moss to plug the hole in his side. Thorne was holding the moss pack in place, part of it forced into the wound, having nothing to tie it off, when the sound of gunshots died on the air, and silence settled over them in its place.

CHAPTER SIXTEEN

"You attract more lead than anybody I've ever seen," Thorne said mildly as he continued to hold the moss bandage in place with his left hand, keeping his gun hand free. His eyes warily slipped back and forth along the snow-covered slope. The sounds of hoofs moving, softly thudding in the snow, reached his ears. He and Scott must be well hidden from view of the riders on horseback.

Sweat popping out across his forehead, Scott grimaced "You reckon I'm gonna make it?"

"You better. I ain't about to tell your sister you give up on me out here." The words were barely out of Thorne's mouth than a horse came up on them fast. He swung around, drawing his gun in the same instant, still managing to hold the makeshift bandage in place.

Angus Mitchell swung down off his horse hurrying to where his son laid in the snow. Without any hurry in him, Thorne returned his gun to its holster like it was Mitchell he was expecting in the first place.

"Give me your neckerchief," Thorne said without greeting, then tied it to Scott's own and used them to tie around Scott's middle holding the moss in place.

136

With the bright-eyed look of a wild man, Angus Mitchell laid a hand on his son's shoulder and looked from him to Thorne. "Where Brandy?" he demanded. "What happened?"

Quickly, Thorne filled him in with what he knew and what he had figured from the tracks in the snow. Then Thorne picked up Scott and carried him to the snow hut. He set to restoking the hot coals of a burned-out fire into a crackling blaze.

"So that's why Harper Manning took what was left of that pack of coyotes he had with him and took out down the mountain," Angus said bitterly. "He'd already checked this here hut and knew she'd taken out. He was waiting to nail you." His face was stormy, his black eyes flat and hard. "We best get after her, Manning is no fool. He knows we can't fight him if he has her."

Thorne shook his head. "Scott can't move 'til we rig a travois and we ain't got time now. You can't leave him alone. He's your son, and he needs you."

"And Brandy's my daughter," Angus snapped; "ain't no man gonna tell me I can't go after her."

"And I'm the man who's going to marry her," Thorne shot back at him. He paused by the hut's entrance, gun in hand, letting his statement sink in. "Besides, one man would have a better chance anyhow. I'll get her back."

Angus started to say something, but Scott reached up and weakly put a hand on his father's arm. "Let him go, Pa," he urged softly. "He's like an Injun in these mountains. He's right, he'll make out."

Looking down at his son's face, Angus saw it to be white and pinched beneath the weathered tan. The shock of the wound was wearing thin, and he was hurting. Finally, Angus turned his worried black eyes on Thorne and nodded without saying a word.

Thorne was out of the hut and down the slope to where the horses had scattered without making a sound in his passing. One thing was certain, Angus had been right in what he said. Thorne had to hurry. There was no way for Brandy to know about the separate party of searchers below, and by now it was certain that Colten had found Pike and turned him loose. Brandy was a smart girl, and she had a good woods sense, but if she came across Pike and Colten, she wouldn't have a chance.

Riding the horse he had stolen from Pike, Thorne kept his rifle out and ready as he started down the trail behind Brandy, Jake moving out ahead of his mount. The big dog was keyed up and ready for trouble, the past couple days honing his fighting instincts to a fine sharpness. He moved with a savage wariness, his green eyes probing into the lengthening shadows cast by the late afternoon sun. Alert, his ears moved constantly, his nose testing the air. But the wind was drifting the wrong way and Jake couldn't catch the scent of Manning's men. But instead, he heard something that stopped him dead in his tracks.

Pulling up sharply behind the big dog, Thorne had his rifle at the ready. The abruptness of his stop was all that saved his life. A shot cracked from somewhere close by, the bullet falling short in the snow at his horse's feet. Startled, the horse half reared. As Thorne forced his mount down and lunged for cover, he heard a second shot, and Jake's piercing yelp of pain. For an instant, Thorne saw the big dog was down, but then he came to his feet, plunging blindly into the trees opposite Thorne. Thorne called softly to the wounded animal, but several well-placed shots kept him pinned, not daring to break cover. If it hadn't been for Jake,

Thorne would have simply slipped back among the trees and kept moving. But that dog had saved his life more than once, and it wasn't in him to leave him behind.

Belly crawling through the snow a ways, Thorne worked his way to where he could see pretty well under the lower branches of the pines. Jake was nowhere in sight, but the snow was dotted with his blood, and Thorne had a pretty good idea where the gunman was. There was no movement, so Thorne started carefully working his way around, trying to come up on him from behind. Once, Thorne thought he heard Jake growl, low and menacing from quite a distance off, in the direction he was heading, but the big dog didn't come to him.

It wasn't too hard for Thorne to work his way up behind Manning's gunman. For some reason, most folks just figured on a body staying in one place. Thorne, though, had different ideas. He was a naturally moving man. If there was one thing his pa managed to teach him during those few hectic years they'd had together, it was to keep his head down and keep moving when trouble showed. Thorne always lived his life by that one simple rule, and he was still walking around to talk about it.

Time passed, more of it than Thorne would have liked, as he worked his way through the snow and trees. When he finally came up on that gunny, he just holstered his gun and pushed his hat back on his head, letting out a long, low sigh. The man was dead, and it wasn't too pretty. Jake had gotten to the man first. It must have happened when he had heard the big dog growl. This was one man who would have been purely sorry he had tried bushwhacking them, if he had lived.

Thorne glanced down at the trampled-down snow.

139

A lot of bootprints and pawprints as well as a trail of blood droplets were in the snow, leading off downslope. As near as Thorne figured, Jake couldn't be thinking too straight. He had been wounded a time or two in the past, but he had always headed back to Thorne, somehow knowing that was where help was.

Turning, Thorne went back for his horse, and started down. That was the direction both Brandy and Jake had taken. He had to find both of them, and fast. A kind of distant chill was clawing at Thorne's insides, and it wasn't from the winter weather that surrounded him. There was snow in the air again, the clouds piling up thick and heavy, blotting out the afternoon sun. He had to find them before the snow hit again, before it had a chance to cover up what tracks he had to follow. Before too, it had a chance to force Brandy into a corner. There was no hiding it, he was worried, but that wasn't something to slow him down none. His horse slipped in the snow once, but Thorne pulled him out of it, and continued on, his face set and determined.

CHAPTER SEVENTEEN

More scared than a calf lost in a stampede, Brandy stayed huddled in the grove of aspen where she had holed up for better than an hour. She heard shots, a lot of them coming from above, in the direction of the hut she had left. The shots echoed on the mountainside, and Brandy shuddered to think of what was happening on the slope above.

When the guns stopped firing that first time, Brandy picked up her rifle and small bag of supplies, and moved on. There was no way of telling what had happened while all that shooting had been going on. One thing was certain, if Thorne was all right he would be coming after her. Brandy knew he would find her. But if Harper Manning was still looking for her, she knew Thorne wouldn't be wanting her to be just sitting in one place waiting for him to show himself.

Brandy was scared. She hadn't ever in her life been as scared as she was now. When Thorne had been with her she had been frightened some, but not like this. Her bright brown eyes combed the slope just outside the fringe of aspen she was moving through. She had no more than started skirting an open, unbroken expanse of glistening white snow than the shooting started again, but this time there weren't so many guns, nor did the shooting last as long. In a small hollow circled by pines, she held up again and glanced nervously in the direction from which she had come. The shooting had been some closer to her than the first. She held her rifle a bit tighter, her knuckles turning white. Just then, she heard a rustling in the brush a short distance from her. Instinctively, Brandy swung her rifle to cover the direction where the sound was coming from. A faint rustling sound reached her ears again, and then some snow plopped softly from one of the lower pine limbs a short distance away. There was a low animal sound, then Brandy caught a glimpse of fur against the whiteness of the snow. She heard the sound again, and Jake limped out into the open, his great, shaggy head swaying from side to side as if he wasn't sure where he was. Instantly, Brandy recognized him, and it was then she saw the wound that had laid open his left foreleg. It made him half wild with pain. Where was Thorne? Brandy's concern was reaching new heights. He wouldn't leave the big dog alone, wounded the way he was, if he could help it.

"Jake," Brandy called softly, "Jake, come to me."

The big dog's massive head turned in her direction, his green eyes seeming vacant. A growl sounded low in his throat. The sound was savage and menacing, then he moved on a few more strides, stiff-legged.

"Jake," Brandy tried again, her voice gentle and reassuring, "come to me, boy."

Half turning toward her, Jake stopped, his green eyes fierce and bright. Panting heavily like he'd been running, he cocked his head as he stared in her direction. He was torn between wanting to be alone with his pain, and wanting the touch of a familiar hand. The voice that spoke quietly from a distance, making no attempt to move closer, was one he had heard before, and somewhere in the back of his mind, he remembered her touch.

Cautiously, limping badly, Jake started across the white expanse in her direction, head lowered, his eyes never leaving her. Brandy held out a hand for him to sniff as he approached, feeling no fear for herself, only pity for Jake He stopped a couple of strides from Brandy, eyeing her cautiously, hesitated another instant, then went to her as if realizing he could expect help from her.

From the clouds that hung about the mountain peaks like black smoke, Brandy knew it was snowing higher up. The temperature was already cold enough for snow where she was, and it would not be long in reaching her. Hurriedly, she did what she could for the big dog, binding his wound, and speaking to him gently as she did. Icy winds drifted off the mountaintops, swirling the top layer of snow about Brandy's feet, but the soft whisper of wind concealed the savageness of the winter storm that was brewing. That she should be moving on Brandy knew, but she was afraid she might be moving away from Thorne. He had to have gone back to the hut by a different trail or she would have run across him by now. And all that shooting. There could be no reason for it other than Manning and Thorne running afoul of each other. Exhausted, and her side aching, Brandy glanced down at Jake lying in the snow at her feet. He couldn't go much farther either. They had to find a place to hole up. The clearing they faced was not large. Brandy decided to cross it, and find a place on the other side. With only a few low words of urging, Jake climbed to his feet and they started across the unbroken snow for the trees on the far side.

Picking his way slowly down the slope, following Brandy's trail, Thorne paused a moment on a rocky outcropping that was swept nearly bare of snow by the wind.

Worry marked every line in his hard face as his blue-gray eyes combed the slopes below hoping for some sign of Brandy. From his place on the outcropping, he could see almost every clearing and bush-enclosed hollow all the way down the mountain as if they were blank spots on a playing board. It took but a few moments for his eyes to adjust to the terrain, to start picking out little things that did not belong. Jake was preying on his mind as well as Brandy. The big dog could cover a lot of country. There was no telling how far he managed to get, providing he was still alive. Thorne reckoned that he was. Jake would take a lot of killing. Hurting the way he was, he would also take a lot of finding if he didn't want to be found.

For a time, Thorne's eyes moved up and down the slope, not really focusing on anything. The snow was drifting lightly to the ground around him, the beginning of the storm that still hung about the far peaks, as if it couldn't dislodge itself to swoop down on the lowlands. Thorne thought about what to try if the snow covered what tracks he had to follow. He was beginning to believe he wouldn't be seeing anything from that rocky outcropping, where his horse pawed nervously at the ground, when the slope below him came alive almost as if he had uttered some magic words.

Below, at what must have been midway between the bottom and where Thorne sat his horse, he spotted a small figure moving out against the whiteness of the snow. It could be no one but Brandy. He watched as she stopped, and half turned, as if waiting for something. Then, from behind the trees that had blocked Thorne's vision, he spotted a huge wolflike bulk limping slowly behind the girl. Jake! Somehow he had worked his way down and joined up with Brandy. Thorne allowed himself a slow smile and started to turn his mount so that he could take out after them when a flash of movement on another part of the slope caught his eye. He pulled his horse up short, frowning as he focused his attention on the movement that had drawn his eye. The rocky outcrop that he had chosen for his lookout was proving to be even more valuable than he'd first imagined.

There, below Brandy, almost at the point where Thorne had managed to get a horse long hours before, Thorne could make out the moving figures of several men. Two of the group had separated themselves from the others and were working their way directly toward Brandy. And, on the slope above, not more than a hundred yards or less was the bunch that had bushwhacked him and Scott back up at the hut. There were plenty of trees down there, and no way for Brandy to be able to tell that she was caught right in the middle of things. To top if off, on the upper slope, at the head of the group a single man rode proud and dressed proper. Thorne didn't need anybody to tell him who that was. It could only be Harper Manning.

With a quick motion, Thorne checked the six-gun that rode easy at his hip. Satisfied, he slipped it back into his holster, and turned his horse back onto the trail. He had never met this Harper Manning face to face, but he had already been jumped by his men twice, and caught in the cross fire at the Mitchell place. What's more, the man had mistreated Brandy, and for that there was no give in Thorne. He had come to his valley to find peace, but he'd run smack up against Manning's greed and found himself fighting one of the most violent battles of his life. It was way past too late to back up now, even if it was in Thorne to do it. There was a coldness in him not caused by the piercing chill of the wind. Thorne had seen a good boy fall, a boy who he had no way of knowing whether he were still alive or dead. He had seen a worried father torn between loyalty to son and daughter, and he'd seen the woman he loved hurt and near dead with exhaustion.

His face was dark and brooding. The calculating violence of a pacing cat lurked quietly within Thorne, waiting to spring, and it was long overdue in being cut free. Impatiently, he put his heels to his horse, urging him to greater speed through snow that, in the hollows, came well above his knees. Thorne's mount, the horse that had a short time earlier belonged to Sonora Pike, hadn't been born to this kind of country, but he was strong and seemed willing to plow into almost anything.

Riding quiet, his lean, hard body sat straight and easy in the saddle. The only sign of the tension that was in Thorne was the strength with which he gripped the reins. Inside his black leather gloves, his knuckles showed white.

CHAPTER EIGHTEEN

An old fallen log was not too far within the stand of pines Brandy had crossed to. Bone weary, she sat down on it, and Jake quickly followed her example, dropping to the snow at her feet. It seemed to her that he was limping worse all the time. He was panting heavily and it was plain he needed some rest. Brandy was taking in air in deep gulps. She wasn't kidding herself, she needed rest as much as Jake did. She hadn't done much more than cat nap for a couple of days, and her side hurt with every breath she drew.

Brandy glanced back over her shoulder at the clearing she and the dog had just crossed. She should have kept to the trees, skirted the clearing. It worried her that in her exhaustion she should make such a mistake. It was possible that someone had seen her. On a mountainside such as this, with only a few clearings, any movement upon one would draw a person's eye like a black spot on a white tablecloth.

Too tired to even notice the tiny, delicate flakes of snow that were drifting down around her, Brandy stayed where she was. It wasn't until she heard a sound close by that she glanced up and saw the white flakes catching on Jake's thick coat. Startled by both the unexpected sound and the arrival of the long-expected snow, she jumped up, her bright brown eyes sharp and questioning. Her raven hair, usually shining, was matted and dull, loosely tied back with a leather string she had earlier cut from that which held their supplies. There was a wild look about her as she held her rifle at the ready and listened.

Sounds of footsteps coming from below reached Brandy's ears, and they were coming toward her fast. There was a chance that it was Thorne, but something warned her that it wasn't. Perhaps it was in the way the footsteps fell, or the sounds they made in attempting to move silently. Jake's head was up, his ears pricked, and a snarl curled his lip. In a whisper, she called the dog to her. Together they moved deeper into the trees and cut their trail off in another direction, going at an angle with the direction they'd been traveling before. Brandy was not nearly so adept at moving silently as Thorne, and sound carries far on the clear, mountain air. She had taken only a few steps when she became aware that the steps that had been moving toward her had also changed their direction. She stopped short, and moved off another way, still working toward the bottom of the mountain. Abruptly, she heard a branch crack, once again the following footsteps had changed their direction. Almost in panic, Brandy pushed on a little faster, Jake limping to keep up beside her, though it was plain it was an effort for the wounded animal to do so.

Keeping the hard pace, Brandy probed the surrounding terrain for some place where she could take to cover and have her back protected. She dodged another fallen limb and was heading for a cluster of boulders when a man, as sudden and quiet as a cougar, appeared on the trail not more than a couple of feet from her. Before Brandy could react, one rough, dark hand darted out from his side and snatched the rifle from her grasp. It took only an instant for her to recognize the man. He was the one who had let her leave Manning's ranch without question, the one who was called Ben Colten.

Almost tripping in the deep snow, Brandy dropped back a step. Colten was not a man to waste time chasing like the other man, the one who had been following her through the snow. He had figured, and he had figured right. He set to reckoning where a wounded animal might go to hide, or to make a last stand. The boulders here, and the trees, they were the best spot he had found. But, he had found the wrong animal. The girl wasn't what he was tracking, it was the man he was after…Thorne Stevens. It was not even a personal matter, for he had no grudge against such a man as Thorne. With Colten, it was a matter of pride. Professional pride. And money.

About the time Jake started his low, menacing growl, Colten's wolfish face broke into a grin. "You best watch that dog, missy," Colten advised softly. "He comes for me, I'll finish him once and for all."

Brandy threw a few quiet words she had heard Thorne use in Jake's direction, her eyes barely leaving Colten for a second. Whether or not the big dog would listen to her when she spoke to him she did not know, but there was no more she could do than try. To her surprise, Jake's ears pricked forward, and he sat back on his haunches at her restraining words. Not knowing what Colten had in mind, Brandy stared questioningly at him.

148

Giving her another slow smile, Colten's cool blue eyes were empty of emotion. Slowly, he unloaded Brandy's rifle, dropping the shells into his own pocket. "If you're a-wonderin' what I'm fixin' to do," he said slowly, "you needn't worry your head about it. You can jest mosey on down this here mountain. I got no call to stop you." The rifle empty, Colten handed it back to Brandy.

Jumpy and uncertain, she gazed at him for long seconds, her soft brown eyes mirroring her worry.

"You get along now," Colten told her again, his tone almost fatherly. "There ain't nothin' to stop you."

The snow crunched behind Brandy and Sonora Pike's voice cracked like a whip across them. "The hell there ain't!" he exploded. "I say she stays right here." He reached out so fast, grabbing Brandy by one arm, that she half fell in the snow, in her attempt to pull away, and a startled scream escaped her lips.

That single, short scream cut Jake loose like a stone hurled from a catapult. With a savage snarl, he jumped for Pike. It happened so fast that Jake was on him before Pike could aim a gun. He turned Brandy loose and was bowled into a drift by the force of the dog's charge before he managed to use the butt of his gun as a club on the already weakened animal. The big dog fell limp as Pike connected on the side of his head.

Pike rolled to his feet, glaring coldly at Colten. "Didn't see you lending a hand," he snapped.

"No need to," Colten retorted, "It was your throat he was goin' for, not mine I was kind of hoping he might make it."

"You look here, old man," Pike said, his voice thick with anger and contempt, "from now on, you

149

do what I say, and nobody else. She's staying right here 'til things settle down. Then, maybe I'll give her to Harper Manning, if I'm a mind to. On the other hand," he sneered, "I kind of took a fancy to her myself. Might just keep her around, tame her down some." He paused, giving Colten an appraising look. "Now, if you don't clear out of here, like the rabbit you are, and never show your face in these parts again, I might just take a notion to finish you off."

A fleck red showed in the depths of Colten's cool blue eyes. "I told you I don't hold with bothering womenfolk, boy," he said slowly, "and I told you I would take you. Looks like now you've gone and made me do it."

The words were barely said, their harsh bite still ringing in Brandy's ears, when the six-guns of both men exploded, spitting flame and lead. The sound rolled down the snowshrouded mountain like the roar of distant thunder.

Thorne's horse was already moving down the slope through the snow faster than was safe when Thorne heard Brandy's short stifled cry. The slope before Thorne was steeper than he would have cared to risk under ordinary circumstances, but he knew Manning to be closer to Brandy than he, and there was no time to find another way. He looked down at the snow-covered slope, not knowing what the feathery snow hid, knowing the risk of not reaching Brandy at all if his already tired horse floundered and fell. The pair of shots from the same direction lent a note of urgency to his ride as Thorne's mount lunged onto the steep slope, cutting first one way then another in a mad scramble to keep all four feet beneath him. Feeling the quivering of the animal's tired muscles as he took the steep slope with fast, choppy strides, Thorne rode as though he was a part of the horse. Thorne rode well, keeping his weight shifted to his mount's advantage and came off the slope below, slipping and sliding, loose snow flying in every direction.

Exhausted, and almost staggering, Thorne's horse took the last few strides into the clearing still at a run. Thorne was half off his horse, his gun pulled before he came to a complete stop only a few strides from where Sonora Pike lay dead in the snow, a bullet through his heart. The smell of gunpowder still hung on the air. Brandy spun around so fast at the sound of Thorne's arrival that she had to catch hold of a tree to keep from falling back into the snowdrift from which she had just picked herself. A look of relief washed across her face as she saw who it was. Thorne's senses were alive to the dangers around him, and what they were telling him wasn't good. He could hear horses approaching fast, and if they were not going to give him enough trouble, Ben Colten half lay in the snow, his steady gaze and his gun trained on Thorne. He had been hit, how hard Thorne couldn't rightly tell, but he was still conscious and staring at him over that gun barrel. The expression in Colten's eyes never changed, and he looked as relaxed lying there bleeding all over the snow as he did on that day back when he had been sitting in Harper Manning's easy chair. Chancing Colten's gun, Thorne went to where Brandy stood, her face white and pinched, her eyes alive with fear and pain. Just beyond her, Jake lay in the snow, his sides moving regularly with his breathing.

Thorne stared intently at Colten, knowing there wasn't much time left for the injured gunman. He knew he couldn't chance being caught out there in the open when the other riders came up with them.

151

Though Thorne still held the gun he had pulled as he dismounted, the barrel wasn't leveled as was Colten's. It would give Colten an edge. Thorne was about to take the chance when that wolfish face broke slowly into one of Colten's rare half smiles.

"You had time enough to recollect me?" he wryly asked Thorne, his voice steady and low.

Thorne nodded.

"And she's your woman." Colten gestured toward Brandy. He chuckled to himself, answering his own question before Thorne had a chance to. "'Course she's your woman. She'd have to be plumb loco to take the chances she did less'n she was." Colten's voice remained calm, his gun hand steady.

The words were no more than out of Colten's mouth than Thorne dove for cover on the edge of the clearing, dragging Brandy with him Ben Colten's gun remained unfired in his grasp, and his sly grin remained fixed on his angular face. He had told Manning he wasn't going to be in on any shooting, and he had meant it, at least where that girl was concerned. He never had taken to shooting with women around, and she was something special besides. Colten's blue eyes stared longingly after Brandy. A few years back, he would have made a play for her himself. But he decided his own style would have been more like Thorne Stevens's than Harper Manning's or Sonora Pike's. Colten was a hard man, but he knew better than to try and win a filly by force. It took sweets and soft talk, at least a gentle way about a man. Painfully, Colten rolled himself to one side and started to work his way into the trees down toward the horses.

CHAPTER NINETEEN

Making no effort to keep their movements quiet, Harper Manning and the five men with him broke into the clearing. One of his men caught sight of Thorne as he went to ground and passed the word by cutting loose with his six-gun. The rest followed his example, peppering the trees with lead above where Thorne and Brandy lay. Thorne stayed where he was, spread out flat in the snow, half covering Brandy and waited out the barrage. It was then Manning yelled something about his men getting themselves into the trees and flushing Thorne out.

During a lull in the gunfire, Thorne gathered himself to move Brandy on out of there. He glanced back at where Colten had been lying in the snow, and saw only a blotch of crimson to show where he'd been. The wound must not have been as serious as it had looked at first. Thorne puzzled some over Ben Colten. Why hadn't he pulled the trigger when they had broke for cover? Even if he had not wanted to hit Brandy, the man was a dead shot, and Thorne knew he could have singled him out with ease. And now, he had disappeared, slipped off somewhere like a wounded animal. A wounded animal, Thorne well knew, was the most dangerous.

As the snow fell lightly around them, Thorne caught the faint sound of voices moving slowly toward them. They were more cautious of him now, like they would be of a wounded bear, but at the same time they would be planning on Brandy slowing him down considerably. Thorne threw a couple of slugs in the direction he figured one or two of them might be, then moved away from where he'd been lying, keeping low, and signaling for Brandy to follow. A few bullets sang nearby, but Thorne knew them to be guessing. Brandy shivered and pulled herself closer to him as the sounds of gunfire cracked around them.

Thorne knew he had to do something. He was a moving man, and wasn't used to being boxed. His blue-gray eyes slipping back and forth beneath the brim of his battered Stetson, Thorne glanced quickly about himself. Light-falling snow was collecting in a little hill in the crease of his hat, and was catching in the disheveled tangles of Brandy's raven hair as she no longer had her hat. A couple of shots came from one side, hitting closer than those before. Gripping his gun tighter, Thorne frowned and moved again, keeping close to the edge of the clearing, but well inside the ring of trees. Brandy stuck close beside him. Fumbling with the shells she had forgotten were still in her pockets, she managed to reload the rifle Colten had emptied.

For a time the guns were silent. The only sounds to be heard were the occasional cracks of twigs beneath the blanket of snow, and the blowing of some horses nearby. Manning and his men were circling them. Thorne could feel it. What was worse, there wasn't anything he could do about it. They knew the general area where he was, and with Brandy he couldn't move fast enough or cover his tracks well enough to slip away. The real irony was the fact that if Brandy wasn't with him, Thorne wouldn't consider slipping past Manning's men in the first place.

Thorne glanced over at where Jake still lay motionless in the snow. If it weren't for the steady rhythm of his breathing Thorne would have thought him dead.

154

The disappearance of Colten preyed on Thorne's mind. Would he fight? Was that wily old wolf working down on them now, or had he crawled off somewhere to tend that wound? It was anybody's guess, and Thorne knew he didn't have any guessing room left. At least seven men were out there, counting Manning himself, and all were enemies. What Thorne did, he knew had to be right, or it would all end there on that mountain slope for him and Brandy. Quickly, while the other guns were quiet, Thorne filled the empty chambers of his gun. Evening was coming on fast, the sun would be setting soon. Already the daylight was turning dusky. If they could hold out, the darkness would make a difference. Thorne was as at home prowling in the night as a big cat.

Gazing intently toward the clearing, combing the farther side for some sign of Manning or his men, a flicker of motion caught the corner of Thorne's eye. Almost too late, Thorne spun around on his knees, slipping in the snow as he instinctively snapped off a shot. His shot missed, and for an instant he caught a glimpse of a thin man, lean and hard-faced with a self-assured grin on his lips. The stranger stood there spraddle-legged gazing at Thorne, making the mistake of savoring what he thought to be his triumph. It happened so fast, Thorne scarcely felt the impact as his fall left him prone in the snow, his gun at the ready, his finger already tightening on the trigger. And in that instant, the gunman, seeing Thorne's gun coming level, realized he'd waited too long. In a panic, he snapped off his shot too fast, and the bullet that had been meant to kill caught Thorne in his left forearm. Thorne had steadied down after the first shock of the man's appearance, and his shot did not miss. A look of pained surprise spread across that hard, dark face, and the smile of triumph faded as he sank to his knees and folded, without a sound, into a low drift.

The shooting started again with renewed vigor, the bullets slamming into trees, and pock-marking the snow around Thorne. He hurriedly pulled himself up to where he could sit with his back against a tree, wrapping his wound with his neckerchief at the same time. Brandy brought her rifle up and returned the fire, hitting nothing, but keeping the others close to cover. After a time, the exchanged slowed, and silence again hung heavy on the air.

"Brandy!" Manning's voice cut through the coming darkness, and the silence like the rasping of an old gate. "Come on out here. There's no reason for you to be mixed up in this."

Leaving Manning's call unanswered, Brandy glanced sideways at Thorne, her gaze questioning what they would do next.

Thorne kept his voice low, barely above a whisper. "I have to go out after them," he told her urgently, "I have to go alone."

Brandy looked frightened, biting her lip nervously as she nodded in answer to what Thorne was saying. Taking Brandy by the hand, Thorne stayed crouched low, and led her farther up the slope. They had not gone more than a few yards when Thorne found what he was looking for. It was a small dip in the earth, hollowed out between the huge roots of an old pine. Small as she was, it was barely large enough for Brandy to squirm down into.

"Stay here, and keep low," Thorne said firmly. "I'll be back for you." He glanced quickly around, memorizing the spot, then slipped off as quietly as an Indian.

Holding her rifle at the ready, Brandy huddled low in the little cup-shaped hole, waiting for the shooting to begin again. The snow she had scooped out of the bottom of the hole to let her fit in surrounded her like a blanket, trapping her own warmth close to her. Brandy noticed that the falling snow seemed to be coming down heavier, then the shooting started again.

Working his way around the edge of the clearing, Thorne made his way back to where Manning and his men had first appeared. He knew what he was after, and it wasn't Manning's hired guns. It was Manning himself. The way to kill a snake was to destroy its head, and that was what Thorne was figuring on doing, one way or another. He'd seen one of Manning's men as he moved, but managed to avoid him. It was when the second one showed that the shooting started again. Thorne's gun was already out when he came almost face to face with the square-shouldered, moon-faced gunman. He had been ready, the gunman hadn't. Thorne fired, hitting the man, and moved on without knowing how bad.

The firing started again, in bursts, coming first from one side, then the other. His head down, Thorne kept moving, answering a shot only when it got too close. The shots were coming closer, they were narrowing down to the places he would have to be, and Thorne was just starting to figure on another direction, when he spotted what he had been looking for. Through the trees he caught a glimpse of a fine leather coat and a gray felt hat that looked to be new. Manning had to be inside fine duds like those.

Thorne glanced quickly around, knowing the only way to reach Manning was to expose himself to the gunfire of his men. His dark face was grim and set, his eyes hard. He had to chance it, he had to figure

157

Manning's men wouldn't risk a shot with Thorne's gun trained on him. That meant he had to be up close, his gun trained on Manning before the others could figure what was happening.

Warily, Thorne eased himself down flat in the snow and started working his way forward on his belly. The snow was deep in places, but he kept moving, plowing through the light stuff as if it was a field of grass. Snow was still falling as Thorne continued to move forward with the quiet of an Indian until he wasn't any more than four or five yards from where Manning had held up behind the thick trunk of an old pine. He could hear the man talking, but couldn't make out the words. Knowing what he had to do, Thorne looked around, sorely aware of how little cover he had. There were trees to his left, one close up beside him, but little else. If something went wrong, he would have to be moving mighty fast to save his skin. Taking his hat off, Thorne raised up enough to get his first good look at Harper Manning. His hawk face was intent, his dark, brooding eyes moving quickly from one place to another. Thorne remained unmoving in the snow while Manning's eyes passed over him as the man searched the edges of the clearing, not letting his gaze settle so near him.

Without warning, the frown deepened on Manning's forehead. From the corner of his eye, he had spotted Thorne, but his mind had refused to acknowledge it until it was already too late. Manning looked again to where his eyes had passed only a few seconds before, and found himself staring into Thorne's cold blue-gray eyes and down the black, cavernous barrel of his Colt Peacemaker. For an instant, Manning felt a crazy impulse to bring his own gun up and cut loose, but cold logic told him he would never get off a shot.

Up on his feet, snow clinging to his clothes, Thorne cocked his gun and took a couple more steps toward Manning. He wasn't more than six feet away from the man when he stopped. From somewhere back in the trees, Thorne thought he heard a muffled cry. It startled him, worried him, but he had gone too far to turn back. His gun was cocked and he was staring Harper Manning in the eye. Thorne's only chance was to bluff it out, and hope Manning had hired only the best gunmen in the territory. Such men would know Thorne would take Manning with him if he went. And though where Thorne stood cover was sparse, there was enough to make a perfect shot almost impossible. An experienced gunman would know Thorne wouldn't shoot at anything else until Harper Manning went down with one of his slugs in him. Thorne was counting on that experience to make them just that much more cautious about where they were slinging lead.

"I'd just as soon kill you as look at you," Thorne coldly informed Manning, "so don't go trying anything. Just drop your gun, easy like, and tell your men to do the same."

Manning cast Thorne a deadly look, his face stiff, his eyes cold. "You're a dead man," he said slowly. "I've got enough men to cut you to ribbons."

Thorne shrugged. "Might be, but if I go down, you're going with me." His weathered face was grim, his jaw set. A dying man could kill, he needed only the split second and determination to do it. And Thorne knew he had that determination. It was hard to read Manning, his coldly handsome face was dark with anger, but for a second it looked to Thorne as if he was going to drop his gun. Then, abruptly, he smiled. A sly, cold look came into his eyes like the chill of the winter wind off the mountain. Thorne didn't have to turn his head to see Brandy at the far edge of the clearing. A man was standing close behind her, holding her right arm tight up behind her back, and bracing one of her feet with his own, forcing her to stand straddle-legged and unable to regain enough of her balance to fight. Her face was ashen, her eyes large and darkly circled.

"Looks like I've got the high card after all," Manning said shortly, his voice filled with anger. "I think you better drop your gun, for Brandy's sake," he added more softly.

His gun steady, Thorne held Manning's eyes with his own. "Don't reckon I will. If I drop this gun, I'm a dead man, just like you said. I figure I still want to take you with me, and Brandy told me she'd rather be dead than with you." Thorne's face remained closed, his emotions hidden within. It was a wild, dangerous bluff he was playing, but there was nothing left to do but play it out.

Manning's cool reserve broke, and his anger lay plain in the open. "If that man moves her arm much more than a couple inches, he'll break it. You figuring on watching that too?"

"If he hurts her," Thorne said flatly, "if she cries out, I'll squeeze this trigger."

For long seconds, silence hung heavy on the air. The tension that held the men was a thing alive. Snow continued falling soundlessly, the wind was quiet, and even the horses, tied a short distance from them, made no sound. Then, like a distant howl of wind, a laugh, almost unearthly in its sound, drifted across the snowy evening air to them. There was a hollow sound to it, almost like an echo in a canyon.

Thorne spotted a couple more of Manning's men standing a short distance off, glancing around, their

160

expressions puzzled. Laughter rolled again from among the trees, but it was hard to pinpoint exactly where it had come from. Half expecting it was some kind of trick, Thorne looked at Manning but could see he was as puzzled and startled as the rest of them.

Then, through the shroud of snow, and the quickly gathering darkness, Ben Colten appeared. Seeming to appear out of nowhere it was almost as if he were a phantom. One instant there was nothing, the next he was there, walking his mount into the clear, still laughing, and apparently not concerned about the guns that bristled around him. If Thorne did not know better, he would have figured the man to be delirious or just plain crazy. Crazy like a fox, that's what Thorne had heard about Ben Colten. Blood was staining Colten's coat where he had been hit by Pike's bullet, and it was already seeping down into his pants, but still Thorne was alert for a possible trick.

Colten pulled his mount up a few feet out in the clearing, a short distance from Brandy. His angular face looked somewhat pinched, and he didn't seem to be sitting on his horse too comfortably, but if that wound was playing hell with his insides, he wasn't letting on. He let his icy blue eyes wander about the clearing, resting a bit longer on Brandy than the rest. Her lips were compressed into a thin white line, and though she could move only a little, Colten guessed she was fighting that man who held her every minute.

He chuckled softly to himself, then, speaking loud enough for them all to hear, said: "You boys sure are making uncommon fools of yourselves." Easing himself in his saddle a bit, he went on conversationally: "You hire on for fighting wages,

161

do no more'n put some fear into a couple of small ranchers, then end up traipsing all over these mountains trying to run down a little gal for your boss there." Colten made a throw-away gesture toward Manning. "Speaking from my own experience, I figure a man holds his woman or he doesn't…and Mr. Manning never did have this gal to begin with." He glanced around, seeing he held their attention, and noticed a couple more men had appeared at the edge of the trees behind Manning. "Never seen the likes of you boys fighting no women before." Taking off his hat, Colten wiped the band and replaced it over his white-streaked hair.

"Snow's falling harder," Colten commented, "why in a few hours, a day maybe, you won't even be able to get down out of these mountains. And it's coming onto night, so you boys are gonna have to make up your minds real quick, what you're figuring to do." He held Manning's eyes with his own as the snow collected in a little hill on his hatbrim. "Just want to let you boys know before I mosey on, that you won't even be getting paid them fighting wages you've been expecting. Harper Manning is a dead man," Colten told them bluntly. "That fella holding a gun on him is right determined, and he's from the same stock as you. He's figuring on taking Manning if any of you try taking him. There ain't one of you here ain't seen the like before. Any of you here don't figure the same as me about Thorne Stevens is welcome to try a shot." Colten gave a sly grin. "If it was me," he went on, "I would figure it was easiest to take what was owed me in horses and cattle from that spread of his and get onto some other job that doesn't have a smell like something gone bad."

Thorne's gun never wavered, but he couldn't

162

believe what he was hearing Colten tell the rest of Manning's hired guns. He was telling them to back off, to take what was due them and move on to greener pastures. There wasn't any reason for it, but all of a sudden Thorne knew it was going to work. The pair off to one side of Manning and a little in the trees hefted their rifles, gave Thorne a lingering stare, and started moving off toward the horses.

They were hard men, cruel men, but they were not fools, and they didn't figure on not getting what was due them. Before Thorne Stevens had showed up, they had been satisfied enough, but right after he showed, the job had gone sour. And now, they were all figuring Ben Colten was right. Thorne was up at close range, his finger already had taken up the slack on that trigger. Harper Manning was a dead man no matter how good a marksman took out Thorne. Odds were that last reflex action of Thorne's would squeeze off his shot.

One by one they left, the last being the one who had held Brandy. Not believing what had just happened, Brandy stood where the gunman had left her, staring toward where Colten still sat his horse in silence. She could feel Colten's eyes on her as she started slowly toward Thorne, and Thorne half turned to meet her.

It was in that instant that something inside Harper Manning snapped. He cursed, the force of his voice exploding on the air and swung his gun on Thorne. Spinning in his tracks, Thorne dropped to one knee and snapped off the shot he had been so near using the past few minutes. Harper Manning's handsome face came apart with surprise and pain as he clutched at his chest like it would somehow stop the bleeding and save his life. Without a sound, he crumpled the snow-covered ground and lay still.

"Said he was a dead man," Colten said levelly. He stared at Brandy for long moments, his wolfish face appearing almost soft, and his icy blue eyes were hooded to hide the emotion in them. Abruptly, he turned his horse and started to ride off.

"Wait!" Brandy called, concern in her voice. "You're hurt. Let me help you."

"I surely do thank ya', ma'am," Colten said softly without turning back to face her, "but I reckon I'll manage." He touched his heels to his horse, and neither saw the soft smile that hung about his lips as he rode out.

It wasn't until then that Thorne remembered a story he had heard some time back about Ben Colten. It was something about his wife being taken some years ago, stolen like so much baggage, and money demanded for her return. The story said Colten had paid the money, but his wife had never been sent back to him. Being the kind of man he was, Colten had never stopped looking for her, and the men who had taken her from him. Was it just a story like so many other stories about Western men? Or had Brandy's being mixed up in this somehow touched him. Thorne's gaze lingered on Brandy as she crossed the clearing to him and wondered.

"I don't understand him," she said when she reached Thorne's side, "he's hurt, he may die."

"Can't make him stay," Thorne shrugged, "he's a mountain man. I reckon he'll make out."

Jake stirred in the snow behind them, struggling stiff-legged to his feet, his head hanging low, and his face questioning. For a few moments, his luminous green eyes seemed blank, then recognition appeared, and he wagged his tail tentatively, looking from Thorne to Brandy whining softly.

Sympathetically, Thorne gave the big dog a pat

and a few words of encouragement. At the same time he could not help thinking about Brandy's brother Scott and her father farther up the mountain. Night was settling in fast, and the snow was getting heavier. He went for the horses, then quickly told Brandy what had happened, knowing she would have to know the truth.

They were ready to ride when Jake growled, letting them know someone was nearby. Thorne's six-gun came back into his hand like it was an extension of his arm, and he moved in front of Brandy. In the deep shadows, Thorne could make out the figure of a man walking toward them, leading a horse.

"I know you've got a gun pointed at my belly," Angus called hoarsely, "but you can holster it, I'm coming peaceable." Leading his horse, Angus came out of the shadows and Thorne saw that the horse was dragging a travois with Scott riding on it.

Brandy ran through the snow and dropped in the snow at her brother's side. Scott was looking mighty peaked, but he was conscious, and smiling at his sister.

"Couldn't wait around up there!" Angus barked. "Hell, this mountain will be running twenty feet deep in snow in some places afore the week is out."

Thorne took a deep breath of the cold mountain air and sighed with relief. It looked as if they were all going to make it.

We hope that you enjoyed reading this
Sagebrush Large Print Western.
If you would like to read more Sagebrush titles,
ask your librarian or contact the Publishers:

United States and Canada

Thomas T. Beeler, *Publisher*
Post Office Box 659
Hampton Falls, New Hampshire 03844-0659
(800) 251-8726

United Kingdom, Eire, and
the Republic of South Africa

Isis Publishing Ltd
7 Centremead
Osney Mead
Oxford OX2 0ES England
(01865) 250333

Australia and New Zealand

Australian Large Print Audio & Video P/L
17 Mohr Street
Tullamarine, Victoria, 3043, Australia
1 800 335 364